Winner of the Tig Ripley: Rock 'n' Roll Art Contest

Original graphic art provided by Emilie Gray, Duncanville Middle School.

Tig Ripley, Hard Rock

Text copyright © 2017 Ginger Rue

Cover illustration by Amanda Haley

Sleeping Bear Press™

2395 South Huron Parkway, Suite 200, Ann Arbor, MI 48104
www.sleepingbearpress.com
© Sleeping Bear Press

Printed and bound in the United States.
10 9 8 7 6 5 4 3 2 1

Library of Congress Cataloging-in-Publication Data
Names: Rue, Ginger, author.
Title: Hard rock / written by Ginger Rue.
Description: Ann Arbor, MI : Sleeping Bear Press, [2017]
Series: Tig Ripley; book 2 | Summary: "After starting an all-girl rock band with her
middle-school friends, thirteen-year-old Tig Ripley struggles to maintain
control as leader amid band member crises and boy trouble"-- Provided by publisher.
Identifiers: LCCN 2016026742
ISBN 9781585369478 (hard cover)
ISBN 9781585369485 (paper back)
Subjects: | CYAC: Rock groups--Fiction. | Interpersonal relations--Fiction.
Leadership--Fiction. | Popularity--Fiction. | Middle schools--Fiction. | Schools--Fiction.
Classification: LCC PZ7.R88512 Har 2017 | DDC [Fic]--dc23
LC record available at https://lccn.loc.gov/2016026742

For Bryan and Carolyn—Long live the Weathers Mafia

Tig Ripley

Hard Rock

★ GINGER RUE ★

PUBLISHED BY SLEEPING BEAR PRESS

Chapter One

"I can't believe your mom made you wear a dress," Robbie said to Tig.

"I know," Tig replied. "But she kept saying, 'It's not every day my daughter is on TV. You should dress for the occasion.'"

"But the occasion is that we're rock stars!" Robbie said. "That's why we're on TV."

"We're on TV because my uncle's advertising students won nationals with our fake commercial," Tig said. "I wouldn't exactly call us rock stars yet."

"Speak for yourself," said Robbie. She grinned, and

Tig couldn't help but laugh.

"I'm pretty sure you were born a rock star," Tig said.

Robbie nodded and smiled. "Got that right!" She high-fived Tig.

"Be quiet, y'all," Kyra said. "Did you not just hear the guy say, 'Quiet on the set'?"

"Mom? Is that you?" Robbie said. "You look so different these days."

Kyra scowled and sat up straight. When the man counted down three, two, one and pointed, the show's host said, "Good morning, Tuscaloosa! I'm Carolyn Kirk, your host, coming to you live from the College of Communication at the University of Alabama. Thanks, as always, for waking up with us today. This morning we have some very special guests with us: Paul Ripley, Professor of Advertising here at UA, and his students from this year's Ad Comp team. The team is just coming off their latest national victory. Professor Ripley, can you tell us a little bit about what the competition entails?"

As Tig's uncle Paul and his students explained how

they'd first won regionals at the end of the last school year, followed by taking nationals barely a week ago, Tig, Robbie, Kyra, Olivia, and Claire stood to the side, off-camera, waiting to be called over.

"They're calling us up after the clip," Tig said. "Get ready."

After the short clip of the fake commercial with Tig's band playing a seventies punk song to sell ugly, high-waisted pants—a product that had been invented entirely to make the advertising students' job difficult—Carolyn Kirk said, "Wow! That is some commercial! And I understand that these young rock stars are here with us today?"

"They certainly are," Tig's uncle said. "May I introduce you and your viewers to the girls of Pandora's Box?"

"Go!" The man who had counted down a few minutes before now whisper-shouted to Tig and the other girls.

The lights were so bright, Tig couldn't help but squint. The advertising students had given up their seats for the band and gone off-camera. Tig and her friends sat down in the chairs next to her uncle Paul.

Carolyn Kirk introduced the girls by name, along with which instrument each one played. They waved and smiled when their names were called.

"So, tell me, ladies," said Carolyn Kirk, "how does it feel to be famous?" She looked directly at Tig.

"I wouldn't exactly call us famous—" Tig said.

"Yet," Robbie interjected.

Carolyn Kirk laughed. "I see you have some ambition here, huh? That's great."

It sounded so condescending that Tig immediately felt embarrassed, but Robbie didn't seem to feel that way at all. Instead she held her two middle fingers down with her thumb and sort of fist-pumped.

"All right, then," said Carolyn Kirk. "What's next for Pandora's Box?"

"The sky's the limit!" said Kyra, smiling right at the camera.

Olivia and Claire never said a word. They seemed nervous.

"How exciting!" said Carolyn Kirk. "I'm sure I speak for all our viewers in the Tuscaloosa area when I say we wish you the best of luck and look forward to hearing more from Pandora's Box in the very near future!"

Cheesy music began playing, and Carolyn Kirk said, "Coming up next, we'll teach you how to take your grandma's lasagna recipe to the next oh-so-delicious and cost-effective level! Don't go away! We'll be right back!"

"Thanks, Professor Ripley. Thanks, girls," Carolyn Kirk said as the countdown guy whisked them off the set. The entire interview had lasted all of about three minutes total.

"I've got to get some papers graded," Tig's uncle said. "If your mom's not here to pick you up in the next few minutes, let me know. I'll just be right upstairs in my office."

"We'll be fine," Tig said. She hugged her uncle good-bye, and the girls went outside to wait for Tig's mom.

" 'The sky's the limit'?" Tig said to Kyra. "What was that all about?"

"It's called media training," Kyra said. "My mom taught me everything she knew from being in the Miss Alabama pageant. Did I ever tell y'all she was third runner-up?"

"Yes," Robbie said. "I believe you've mentioned it about eighty-seven times."

"Well," Kyra said, "she showed me how to look poised on camera, and she said you're always supposed to say something energetic and fun. The judges love that."

"There were no judges, Kyra," Tig said. "We weren't in a pageant."

"At least I didn't mumble and squint the whole time," Kyra replied.

"Can we go get ice cream?" Olivia asked. "Text your mom and ask if we can meet her at that little place on the Strip. We could walk over there in less than five minutes."

"Olivia's hungry," Robbie said. "What a shock."

The girls were always joking about Olivia's insatiable appetite and her twiggy frame.

"Two words," Olivia said. "*Waffle. Cone.* What are we waiting for?"

The girls agreed, so Tig texted her mom to pick them up at the ice cream shop.

Robbie and Tig hung back while Olivia, Claire, and Kyra walked a few feet ahead.

" 'The sky's the limit'?" Robbie asked. "Your cousin does realize that she can play all of two songs on the bass, right? And even those not very well?"

"Don't look at me," Tig said. "I never know what's going to come out of Kyra's mouth."

"Who knows? Maybe this will inspire her to practice more," Robbie said. "I can hardly wait to get back to the studio and start practicing. Maybe Kyra put in some time on the bass this week. Maybe she's about to blow us all away."

"Maybe," said Tig. But she very much doubted it.

Chapter Two

After ice cream, the girls piled into Mrs. Ripley's minivan and rode to Tig's house. They changed clothes — Tig couldn't wait to get out of that dress and back into her usual jeans and a tee — and went to the studio, which was really just a small building on Tig's family's property.

"Ooh, I have something for y'all!" Kyra said. She opened her backpack and took out five file folders. Each was a different color with a different pattern. She handed one to each girl. "I took the liberty of making everyone a band folder," she said. "Inside you'll find a calendar for the rest of the year, with each practice date in aquamarine type, and monthly band sleepovers at Tig's in marigold yellow. Also, you'll find a current set list in coral."

"Pretty!" Olivia said.

"Look, she even used a label maker for the folder tab!" Claire added. The labels said PANDORA'S BOX.

"You sure went to a lot of trouble," Robbie said.

"I wanted them to look nice," Kyra said.

"Thanks, Kyra," said Tig. Everyone else did the same. "Now, let's get to practicing, shall we?"

They were only a minute into the song before it fell apart. "Hold up," Robbie said. "I'm sorry, but, Kyra, you're killing me. You're in the wrong key again."

"No, I'm not," said Kyra.

"Yes, you are," Tig said.

"Should the rest of us just change the key?" Olivia asked. "Maybe that would be easier."

"I don't think I can sing it in that key," said Claire. "Sorry, Kyra."

"I don't know what y'all are complaining about," Kyra replied. "I am so *not* in the wrong key!"

Robbie put down her guitar and went over to work with Kyra on the bass. Meanwhile, Tig set down her drumsticks, and Olivia took her hands off the keyboard. Olivia, Claire, and Tig looked at one another. They were all having the same thought: *What are we going to do with Kyra?*

"Okay, let's try it again," Robbie said, putting her guitar strap back on her shoulder.

The girls ran through the song again. This time Kyra played in the correct key. But she started acting really weird, popping and slapping the bass during the chorus. "Kyra, what was that?" Tig asked.

"Isn't it cool?" she said. "My dad was watching an Earth, Wind & Fire concert on TV, and I saw their bass player do this stuff, and I wanted to try it."

"You do realize that we are playing music in a genre that doesn't even remotely resemble funk, don't you?" Robbie asked.

"So?"

Robbie sighed. "So, in other news . . . ," Robbie began. Tig was glad she'd changed the subject. Every time the band practiced, Tig feared that Robbie would finally let loose on Kyra about her lackluster bass playing. "What about my request to add a rhythm guitarist?" Ever since they'd made the fake commercial a few months before, Robbie had been lobbying to add another girl to the band. She had a point. Much of the band's success relied on her, since she was the best musician they had—well, unless you considered Claire's kick-butt voice an instrument, which Tig totally did.

Tig kind of suspected that one of the reasons Robbie wanted to add a rhythm guitarist was so she could have the luxury of showing off a little bit as lead guitarist. Tig couldn't really blame her: if she had been Robbie Chan, she probably would've wanted to show off at least a little bit too.

"I'm not opposed to the idea," Tig said. "But where are we going to find one?"

"Yeah, it was tough enough just to get y'all," Kyra said.

"And we all agreed . . . no boys allowed," said Olivia.

"Yeah, Chan," Tig said. "There's kind of a limited

number of girl musicians in Tuscaloosa."

"In Tuscaloosa County, yes," Robbie said. "But I've got this friend from camp. She's from Pickens County, and she's supercool. Name's Paris Nichols. Pickens isn't so far that it couldn't work. And she'd be down if we asked; I'm sure of it."

"And she plays guitar?" Olivia asked.

"Well," Robbie said, "she took lessons in third and fourth grade, but she didn't really stick with it. But since she has some background, I'm sure I could teach her. Paris's really smart and she could learn fast."

Tig wasn't so sure about this. It would've been one thing to bring in a guitarist who could already play. But to bring in someone who was practically a novice and who'd have to come all the way from Pickens County every single time? That was a half hour outside of town.

"Just meet her," Robbie said. "She's so awesome. You'll love her."

Tig was a little surprised that Robbie was so impressed with a girl from the country. As far as Tig knew, a lot of people out in Pickens County had actual farms, with actual livestock and stuff. Robbie, whose folks had moved her here from New York, was so cosmopolitan. It struck Tig as odd that Robbie was so taken with this Paris character.

"Okay," Tig said. "Bring her to our next practice. Does she have a guitar?"

"Does she have a guitar?" Robbie laughed, then got serious. "That's actually a good question. I'll tell her to get one if she doesn't."

Great, Tig thought.

Soon the girls packed up their instruments, and the mom vans/SUVs began arriving for pickup. "Whose car is that?" Olivia asked.

The girls looked outside to see Kyra's dad's red Alfa Romeo, the vintage sports car he'd bought a few months ago but rarely drove.

"Uncle Nick busted out the spy mobile?" Tig asked. She'd always thought it looked like a car from one of those sixties movies with the British secret agents.

"Yeah, Mom's had a lot going on lately," Kyra said. "She has this friend out of town who's been really sick, so she's been gone a lot. Mom's never liked the car, so Dad uses it whenever she's away."

Tig walked to the door with Kyra and waved to Uncle Nick. He waved back but didn't make any effort to get out of the car and chat. Tig found this a bit odd, since Uncle Nick was usually so personable.

Robbie was the last one to leave. "Ripley," Robbie said, "I don't want to cause a family rift for you, but seriously."

"I know," Tig replied. "Kyra stinks. But what am I supposed to do? I can't just boot my cousin out of the band."

"Do you think she really even *likes* playing in the band?" Robbie asked. "I mean, she doesn't seem to enjoy it at all, and she's always complaining."

"Oh, trust me, I *know*," Tig said. Whenever Tig had to scold Kyra about not practicing, she'd launch into a whine that would completely wear Tig out.

"So, if she doesn't like being a musician, why is she doing it?"

"You know why," Tig said. "'The sky's the limit!'

Kyra doesn't want to be a musician. She wants to be a celebrity."

Ever since the fake commercial, Pandora's Box had become B-list local celebrities of a sort. They weren't exactly up there with the UA football coach, but their picture had been in the paper, and with that day's local news show appearance, popularity-wise, they were gaining on the old guy who did the commercials for the local Chevrolet dealership.

"Well," Robbie said. "If she'd put half as much effort into practicing her instrument as she does making cutesy little folders, she might improve. I just don't know how much longer we can keep up this charade of her being our bass player. She's either got to get with it or get gone."

"You're right," Tig said. Of course Robbie was right. But that didn't make it any easier. "I'll talk to her one more time about getting serious about her instrument."

"Good luck," Robbie said.

"Thanks," Tig said. And, boy, was she going to need it.

Chapter Three

Tig went back into the studio and played a little more before she went to her room. Even though she practiced every day and loved trying to pick out new beats from songs she liked, she probably played a little longer than usual so she could delay calling Kyra.

"What's up?" Kyra said when she answered.

"Nothing," Tig said. "I was just playing around with some new beats. We're going to have to learn more oldies songs if we want to be marketable for the grown-ups' party circuit."

The girls had discussed this as a band a couple of

times. If they wanted gigs, they had to be reasonable about what they could actually do. As eighth graders, they were too young to play college parties or bars (like their moms would probably let them do that even if they were thirty!), so the only options left to them were private celebrations and school dances. Some of their parents' friends had asked if they'd play their parties. Tig suspected that they thought it was cute to have a bunch of little girls playing instruments. But the band still needed a few solid set lists, and if they were going to play to the middle-aged crowd, they'd have to appeal to their musical tastes. It wasn't too bad, really. Tig liked some of that old music. Robbie did too. In fact, she liked Led Zeppelin better than just about anything, and they were from the sixties or seventies. But their stuff was pretty hard—hard rock and hard to play. Especially for Kyra.

"Don't you ever get sick of banging on the drums?" Kyra asked.

"No, not really," Tig said. "In fact, I wish you would practice your bass half as much as I practice drums. It would really help the band."

"I *do* have a life outside of the band," Kyra said.

Her tone irritated Tig. First of all, what life did she have outside the band? She wasn't on any teams or anything, and all her friends were in their band, even though Tig knew Kyra would've preferred to hang out with the cooler crowd if they'd have her, but they wouldn't. And second of all, really? *Really? Um, do not give me your attitude when everyone else in the band would have kicked you out a long time ago if it weren't for me!* Tig thought. That was why Tig didn't bother to sugarcoat what she said next: "Kyra, you're going to have a whole lot *more* life outside the band if you don't start practicing."

"What is that supposed to mean?"

"It means you'd better keep up," Tig said.

"Or what?"

"Or you'll leave us no choice but to"—Tig hesitated— "to make other arrangements."

"Are you threatening to kick me out of the band?" Kyra asked.

"I'm not threatening anything," Tig said. "I'm just telling you how it's going to be."

"I can't believe you want to kick me out of the band!" Kyra said.

Ugh! She made Tig want to scream! *How could any human being be so completely frustrating?* Tig thought.

"Kyra!" Tig shouted. "You think I *want* to kick you out of the band? Is that what you think? If I *wanted* to kick you out of the band, I wouldn't have been biting my tongue until it about fell off for the past six months! I wouldn't have been bending over backward to try to smooth over your sorry playing with the rest of the band! I wouldn't have been constantly apologizing to the other girls about your intense level of couldn't-care-less playing so that they would let me keep you around!"

"The other girls want me out of the band?"

Had Tig really said that? She was so mad, she couldn't really remember what she'd just said.

"It's not that," Tig said. "We all want you in the band. We just want *you* to *want* to be in the band."

"I do want to be in the band," Kyra said.

"Yeah, Kyra, but you don't want it for the right reasons and you don't want it when it counts."

"What are you trying to say?"

"I'm saying that you want to be in the band when our picture's in the paper or when everyone's telling us our video was cool . . . or when you can tell people, 'Oh, look at me; I'm in a band.' But day in, day out? The boring parts? The hard work parts? You don't want it then. You just want all the perks without the work. But it's the work that makes the perks possible." Works, perks, possible. Quite a tongue twister.

"That's not true," Kyra said.

"Kyra, come on," Tig said. "How often do you actually practice?"

"I come to all the practices."

"You know what I mean. I mean, how often do you practice on your own?"

There was a long pause. "Pretty much never," she said.

Tig sighed. "Can you work on that for me? For the band?"

"I guess so," Kyra said.

"Thanks," Tig replied.

When Tig got off the phone with Kyra, she felt a little better . . . at first. The conversation had started out on a course to Tig's kicking her out of the band and resulting in bad blood in their family, so Tig was glad she'd avoided that. But the more she thought about it, the more she realized that all she'd really accomplished was . . . nothing. The two cousins had had almost the same conversation several times since the band had been formed. Tig would fuss at Kyra for not practicing, Kyra would make excuses, then promise to try harder, but when it came to the next practice, it would be obvious that she hadn't tried harder at all. Lather, rinse, repeat. Same old routine, over and over.

This could end up getting ugly, Tig thought. She figured she'd better warn her parents before she did anything drastic. When she went downstairs, she found both of her parents in the kitchen, but they didn't hear her come in. They were standing close to each other and whispering, but not in a sweet way.

More like an angry way.

"I wouldn't put up with it for one second," her mom was saying. "Does she think we were born yesterday?"

"Now, Julie," her dad was saying. "Let's not jump to conclusions. We don't know anything for sure."

"Oh, come on!" her mom said. Then Mr. Ripley noticed Tig. He put his hand on her mom's shoulder.

"Hi, Tigger," her dad said.

"Hi, sweetie," said her mom.

Something was weird. Tig could feel it. "Is everything okay?" she asked her parents.

"Of course!" her mom replied quickly. "Everything is fine!"

Tig was skeptical. "Are y'all fighting?"

"Fighting?" Tig's dad said. "No, sweetie. Of course not. We were just having a discussion."

"About what?" Tig asked.

"Nothing you need to worry about," said her mom.

"Are you sure y'all aren't fighting?" Tig said.

"If we were fighting," Tig's dad said, "would I do this?" He grabbed Tig's mom, dipped her like they do in a tango, and kissed her passionately. Then he swung her back up next to him.

"Gross!" Tig said. Her parents giggled.

"I don't think she's convinced," said her mom. "Dave, you'd better do it again."

"No!" Tig said. "Please don't! Forget I said anything!"

As Tig left the room, her parents were still giggling. Obviously, if they'd been fighting, it wasn't too serious. But something was up.

In any case, this was no time to bother them with her Kyra problems. She'd try them later. For now this was all on her.

Tig knew deep down that, as much as she hated to think about it, she and Kyra—and possibly the whole family by default—were headed toward a huge blowup. Unless Kyra suddenly changed, Tig was going to have no choice but to kick her out of Pandora's Box.

Chapter Four

"So, did you talk to Kyra?" Robbie asked Tig the next morning at school.

"Yeah," Tig said.

"And?"

"And she promised she'd try harder."

Robbie looked at the ceiling, smiled, and shook her head.

"I know," Tig said. "I know. But what can I do? She's my cousin."

Robbie shrugged. Tig wanted to change the subject. "How about you?" she said. "Did you talk to your friend from Pickens County?"

"Paris? Yeah. Sorta. I texted her yesterday. She said she'd call me tonight."

"Cool," Tig said. But she wasn't sure she actually thought it was cool. Recruiting another beginner didn't sound like a way to improve their situation. And hadn't Robbie told her that Paris didn't really play guitar much at all? A few lessons years ago? What if they wound up with another Kyra on their hands? Wasn't one enough?

"Tig, Robbie! Look!" Olivia called. Her locker was across the hall from Tig's. She was carrying a purple piece of paper. "Look at this! It's from Will. He put it in my locker before I got to school this morning. Or after I left yesterday. I don't know which. But anyway, look how sweet!" She held out the paper for them to read. *Hoppy International Rabbit Day*, it said. *Love, Will*. He'd drawn a picture of a bunny. It was pretty cute.

"And look, he got you the little organic bunny crackers to go with it," Robbie said.

"Actually, those were from Kyra," Olivia said.

"Does everyone know it's Rabbit Day but me?" Tig asked.

Olivia laughed. "No, it was just a coincidence. Kyra had some of those in her lunch the other day and let me try one. I really liked them, so she got me my own bag."

That was just like Kyra. She could drive Tig crazy sometimes, but she was ridiculously thoughtful. She was always doing stuff like that.

"But you see what he did there, with the card?" Olivia asked. "He said *hoppy* instead of *happy*. *Hoppy* International Rabbit Day. Isn't that just beyond adorable?"

"You guys are sickening," Robbie said. "Aren't they, Ripley?"

"Yeah. Sickening," Tig said. She wondered if Robbie, all kidding aside, actually felt kind of physically sick about the whole thing, because Tig did. Just a mild, passing nausea. Nothing too serious.

"Oh, wait until y'all get boyfriends," Olivia said. "You won't think it's so sickening then." Her eyes got big, as though a lightbulb had just gone off over her head. "Ooh! That's it! Let's find boyfriends for everyone in the band!"

Robbie laughed. "Yeah, I'm gonna devote my life to *that* quest."

"I'm serious! Y'all, it's so fun! I love having a boyfriend!"

"Stop," Robbie said. "Don't be one of those."

"One of those what?" Olivia said.

"One of those . . . boyfriend girls," Robbie replied.

"Boyfriend girls?" Olivia said.

"Yeah, you know . . . those girls who think they have to have a boyfriend all the time or the whole world stops spinning. Those girls who talk nonstop about nothing else but their boyfriend and can't go anywhere without him and all that junk. It's so pathetic."

"It's not pathetic to have a boyfriend," said Olivia.

"No," said Robbie. "It's just pathetic if that's what you're all about. If you're, you know, a boyfriend girl."

"She has a point," Tig said. "I mean, there is more to life than boys."

"Well, yeah," said Olivia. "Of course there is. But

that doesn't mean having a boyfriend isn't a total blast. I mean, what's so wrong with a cute boy leaving a picture of a bunny rabbit in your locker? Say what you will, but I might just be on the lookout for your perfect matches."

"Oh, joy," Robbie said.

"How about you, Tig?" Olivia asked. "Any special requests for your soul mate?"

"I don't believe in soul mates," Tig said. "And if I did, I doubt I'd find mine in middle school."

"You never know," Olivia said. "I wonder who Kyra would like."

"Yes, focus your energies on Kyra. She'll be all over this," said Tig.

"Ooh, there's Claire," Olivia said. "I'm going to pick her brain about her perfect match too." Olivia ran off to catch Claire before homeroom.

"So, Ripley," Robbie said. "*Are* there any guys in middle school who might tickle your fancy?"

Tig made a *pfft* sound. "Not likely," she said.

But that wasn't entirely true.

Chapter Five

There was one particular guy at Lakeview Heights Middle School who tickled Tig's fancy quite a bit.

Problem was, it was Will, Olivia's boyfriend. Olivia's boyfriend, thanks in large part, to Tig herself. She'd fixed them up.

She could kick herself just thinking about it. Will had liked *her*, not Olivia, but Tig knew how much Olivia liked Will, so Tig had played matchmaker.

And now that the two of them were a couple, it made Tig die a little inside every time she saw them together or Olivia told her about some other sweet, wonderful thing Will had done for her.

But Tig was resolved. It was a mind-over-matter kind of thing: she would just force herself not to like Will. She would ignore his gorgeous blue eyes that looked ever bluer when he wore that one particular smoky-blue shirt. She would look away when he grinned that special grin that he seemed to reserve only for her and that made her stomach flip. She would not ponder how smart he was when he answered a really hard question in algebra, nor how sweet he was when he took up for anyone, no matter who it was, whenever people would say something negative about him or her. She just wouldn't think about any of that. And soon she'd be over liking Will.

"What's up, Anti-gone?" Will said when she got to algebra class. Funny . . . last year, it had annoyed her when he'd purposely pronounced *Ann-TIG-ah-nee* wrong. But this year she sort of liked that he called her something no one else did.

"Nothing," Tig replied, forcing herself not to look into his blue eyes. "Saw your rabbit picture."

"Oh," Will said. He seemed embarrassed. "Yeah, I was just trying to make Olivia smile."

"You succeeded," Tig said. "But then again, you always do. She's a pretty big fan of yours."

Was Will blushing?

"Hey, did you do the homework? What'd you get for that last one?" Why was Will asking her that? He certainly didn't need help with algebra. Tig wondered if he just wanted to avoid talking about Olivia with her.

Tig opened her binder and looked at the problem. "I got x equals forty-five," she replied.

"Oh yeah, me too," Will said. "Good to know."

"If this class is as boring today as it was yesterday, please just pack me in a suitcase and send me to Siberia," Regan said. She'd just come in, and she tossed her backpack onto the chair in front of Tig. Tig laughed. Last year she would have made some smart remark about how she would gladly have shipped Regan Hoffman off on a one-way trip to Siberia. But that was seventh grade, and since the eighth-grade year had begun, Regan had been pretty okay. It was almost as though she wanted to be friends with Tig. Weird.

"Siberia?" Tig replied. "Only if you promise to take me with you."

Class was as boring that day as it had been the day before. But it really didn't matter, because Tig wasn't paying that much attention to the lesson anyhow.

All she could think about, no matter how hard she tried not to, was Will.

Chapter Six

Maybe thinking about Will all the time was why, at the salad bar later that day at lunch, Tig put chocolate pudding on top of her green salad with ranch dressing. The desserts were at the end of the salad bar line, and there were separate little plates, of course, for the pudding and cookies, so what was Tig thinking?

"Sheesh!" she said. "What is wrong with me today?"

"That looks not exactly de-lish," said a voice behind her. Tig turned to see Regan. "I don't think that combo is going to catch on." Regan's two besties, or as Tig thought of them, Bots, were not glued to her as usual but were instead sitting at the cool table where Regan's spot was secure.

"Yeah," Tig said. "I'm probably gonna need to scrape that off. I don't know where my head is."

"I bet I do," Regan said.

Tig caught something odd in the tone of Regan's voice. She looked at her quizzically. "What do you mean?"

"I mean, somebody has a bad case of Willingitis."

Willingitis? What was . . . oh no. No, no, no, no, no!

"I don't know what you're talking about," Tig said, perhaps a little too quickly.

"Come on," Regan said. "It's so obvious. I can't believe your little friends haven't already caught on."

"Nobody's caught on to anything because there's nothing to catch on to," Tig said.

"Chill out, Tig. I'm not going to tell anybody. Your secret is safe with me."

"I don't *have* a secret!"

"Oh, please. Let's be real for a second here. I have algebra with you two. The electricity between you and

Will could charge my phone for a week."

"Look, Regan," Tig said. "I don't know what you think you're seeing, but Will and I are just friends. He's in a relationship with Olivia, and Olivia is one of my best friends."

"I know. That's probably what makes it so electric. Forbidden fruit always tastes sweeter. Am I right?"

"No!" Tig said. "I mean, I don't know. I don't know what forbidden fruit tastes like because Will is not a fruit and I'm not . . . I don't even know what to do with your metaphor. You're confusing me."

Regan laughed. "You can deny it all you want, but you should see your face right now. You are, like, fire-truck red. You'd better take a few deep breaths before you go back to your table, or people are going to start asking questions—and you do *not* want that. Not if you want to keep your secret."

"I already told you, I don't have a secret!"

"Yeah," Regan said. "Keep telling yourself that. Maybe you'll start to believe it."

Regan went back to the popular table, and Tig

spooned the lettuce pieces with pudding on them into the trash can. Then she went to her own lunch table. The one with Robbie, Kyra, Claire, and, of course, Olivia and Will.

"Why are your hands shaking?" Kyra asked when Tig sat down.

"My hands are not shaking!" Tig snapped.

"Whoa! Who chapped your hide?" Kyra said.

"Nobody. My hide is just fine. Eat your lunch."

"Are you okay, Tig?" Claire asked gently. "Is something wrong?"

Tig forced a smile. "Sorry, y'all. I guess I'm a little on edge. My algebra grade is kind of bad, and I've got to keep my grades up or you know my parents will ground me from band practice. We don't want that to happen." In truth, her grade was just fine, but Tig thought the little fib was harmless enough.

"I could help you with algebra, if you want," Will said.

"Nah, don't trouble yourself," Tig said. "I'm fine."

"Oh, but Will is so great at algebra!" Olivia said.

"He'd be glad to help you!"

"I couldn't ask you to do that," Tig said. "Really."

"I don't mind," Will said.

"Then it's settled," Olivia said. "Tig, Will is going to tutor you in math, and we won't hear another word about it! We've got to keep those grades up if we want Pandora's Box to thrive."

"You know how much I want the band to thrive," said Tig. And she did. More than anything.

But spending more time with Will wasn't likely to help that cause.

At her drum lesson that afternoon, Tig's concentration was shot. "This shouldn't be such a difficult pattern for you at this point," her teacher, Lee, said. "Everything all right?"

"I'm fine," Tig said. "Just a little distracted, I suppose."

"Anything I can help with?"

"I doubt it," said Tig.

"Oh, so it must be boy trouble," Lee said.

Tig blushed. "How'd you know?"

"I didn't. But from the look on your face right now, I'd say it was a pretty lucky guess."

"Don't worry," Tig said. "No boy is going to distract me from my music."

"As far as distractions go," Lee said, "love's one of the better ones."

Tig blushed again, and Lee chuckled. Then he reset the metronome and resumed counting: *one and two and three and four* . . .

Chapter Seven

"**E**xactly how bad is your algebra grade?" Kyra asked that night on the phone.

"It's not *that* bad," Tig said. "I'm in C territory."

"Yeah, but C territory is unstable. One dumb move and you're in D territory."

"Or one smart move and I'm in B territory."

"What if you stay in C? Will your mom ground you?"

"Not for a C. Not if she feels like I'm doing the best I can."

"Well, at least Will is going to help you," Kyra said.

"He's totes smart."

"Yeah," Tig said.

"Aren't Will and Olivia just the cutest couple ever?"

"Cute as a button," Tig said. She hoped the sarcasm in her voice hadn't been as biting as she thought it was.

"Isn't it funny that he started liking her back, after all that time? I mean, she was so hung up on him for so long, and it was like he didn't even know she was alive. Then all of a sudden, coupledom! I guess it just goes to show that persistence pays off."

"I guess so," Tig replied.

"See, that's what I've been trying to tell you all these years. If we just keep on being nice to Regan and her friends, we will eventually wear them down, just like Olivia did with Will."

"I'm not interested in wearing anybody down," Tig said. "Man, Kyra, why do you care so much about being friends with the Bots, anyway?"

"We're never going to be friends with them if you don't stop calling them the Bots!"

"Fine by me," Tig said. "But that's what they are—

little robots with shiny hair and the same uniform. They all do everything Regan programs them to do. It's like Haley and Sofia and the rest of them have never had an original thought in their lives."

"You've got to admit that Regan has been a lot better to you this year," Kyra said.

"Yeah," Tig replied. "I don't get that. Why is she talking to me and stuff all of a sudden?"

"Maybe it's because she likes you," Kyra said.

"Or maybe it's just another one of her plans to try to destroy Pandora's Box," Tig replied. "Have you forgotten that she buddied up to Claire all those months last school year just to try to keep her from singing lead for us?"

"Yes, but now that we're a real band and people think we're cool, Regan wants to be our friend."

"Has she been nice to you?"

"No, not yet," Kyra said. "But I'm sure it's just a matter of time. I mean, I am the bass player."

"About that," Tig said. "Have you been practicing?"

"I've been pretty busy this week," Kyra said.

"Doing what?"

"Well, helping with the laundry and stuff. Mom's been gone so much with her sick friend that it's just been Dad and me. I've been *busy*."

"Get unbusy," Tig said. "By practice Thursday, you need to show some serious improvement."

"Whatever," Kyra said.

"I *know* you did not just 'whatever' me!" Tig said. "You think just because we're cousins, I'm going to keep covering for you, but I'm not. I *will* make the tough decisions if you force me to."

"Okay, okay," Kyra said. "I believe you."

But Tig knew Kyra didn't really take her seriously at all.

Chapter Eight

O livia decided that Will would tutor Tig every Tuesday after school for half an hour in the library. Try as she might, Tig couldn't find a way out of it.

At the first tutoring session, Olivia walked with Will to the library to meet Tig. "She's probably going to be a tough one," Olivia said to Will, right in front of Tig. "You wouldn't believe how hard she fought this whole tutoring idea. She must really hate algebra!"

"Yep," said Tig. "I do hate me some algebra, all right."

"Well, good luck, Will," Olivia said. "Call me later?"

"Sure," Will said.

Olivia left, and Will sat down next to Tig and opened his algebra book. "Did you bring your book with you?" he asked.

"No," Tig said. "Forgot it." She really had forgotten it, but she wished she hadn't.

"You can look on with me," Will said.

He moved the book, and his chair, closer to Tig. His shoulder touched hers. Regan had been right: it felt like an electric shock.

"Okay, these kinds of problems are all about multiple operations," he said.

"Yeah," Tig said. She knew exactly how to work the problems; they were easy, in fact. But she needed to play dumb. "I mean, what do I do first? There are so many numbers and letters."

Will looked at her and narrowed his eyes. "Tig, why are we even doing this?"

"Doing what?"

"Tutoring. Me, tutoring you in algebra? You're as good at algebra as I am."

"No, I'm not," Tig replied. "I'm really having a

tough time."

"Whatever you say," Will said. "Now then, with this one, you have to remember to change the negative to a positive because of the negative sign inside the parenthesis."

They worked on about a dozen problems, Tig feigning ignorance the entire time. It was excruciating to work such easy problems so slowly, but she couldn't tell Will the truth; that she'd lied about her algebra grade in order to cover up being rattled by Regan.

The timer on Tig's phone went off. "That's thirty minutes," she said. "Gotta run."

"Same time next week?"

"You know what? I think I've had a real break-through. It all makes sense now. You really don't have to tutor me anymore."

"Are you sure?"

"Totally. Everything is going to be fine. I know now what I'm supposed to do."

What I'm supposed to do, Tig thought, *is stay as far away from you as possible.*

Chapter Nine

Tig tried her best to convince Olivia that Will was so brilliant, he'd explained all the mysteries of algebra to her in thirty minutes and that no further tutoring would be necessary. But Olivia wouldn't have any of it. "Your grades are too important," she said. "I say we stay with the tutoring at least until the end of the grading period."

Tig had little choice but to go along with it. Once a week until the term was over, it would be just Tig and Will, alone after school in the library for thirty minutes. As if Tig didn't have enough on her mind with the band. She decided to put the whole tutoring problem out of her mind until the next Tuesday. Maybe before then she would find some way to stop liking Will and the problem would be solved. Better to focus on each day as it came.

Tig was already on edge about Thursday's practice because she doubted that Kyra had practiced. She worried about how much longer the other girls would continue to tolerate it, especially Robbie.

But when Robbie showed up, she wasn't alone. She'd brought a girl, who was carrying a guitar, with her.

"Guys, this is Paris," Robbie said. She introduced each girl by name.

"Great to finally meet you," said Tig. But nothing about it felt great. In fact, Tig immediately disliked Paris, just from looking at her. Paris had thick, shampoo-commercial hair loaded with curls that came past her shoulder blades. She was wearing makeup on her eyes, and her jeans clung to curves neither Tig nor any of her friends had yet. Paris looked more like a sixteen-year-old than an eighth grader.

"Nice to meet y'all, too," Paris said. Tig decided she didn't like her voice. She dragged out the *i* in *nice* too much.

"So, tell us about yourself, Paris," Olivia said.

Paris launched into her life story, which Tig found completely boring. She lived on a farm with her parents, brother, and sister, and her hobbies included caring for goats and baton twirling. "I make soap from the goats' milk," Paris said. "It makes your skin really soft. I brought all of you some!" She opened a backpack and pulled out little cellophane-wrapped bars of homemade soap. Some were lavender, some were ivory, and some were swirls of lavender, green, and blue. "I add oils to them to scent them," Paris explained. "And sometimes coloring to make them look pretty."

"Ooh, look! Mine's lilac!" Kyra said, reading a little handwritten tag.

"Mine's vanilla!" said Claire. "How lovely!"

Paris handed one to Tig. "I left yours unscented and dye-free," she said. "Robbie said you had sensitive skin."

"Thanks," Tig said, thinking, *It's not that sensitive.*

Besides, why would she want to bathe with something that had come out of a goat? Gross! Didn't anyone else think it was gross? They didn't seem to. They were too busy oohing and ahhing over their color-swirled, sweet-scented bars.

"Did you say you twirl baton?" Tig asked.

"Yeah," Paris said. "I'm going to try out for majorette next year when I start high school. I hope I make it!"

Tig looked at Robbie. "Aren't majorettes those girls with the big hair and all the makeup who prance around in those skimpy outfits?" Robbie must have forgotten all that. If there was anything Robbie hated, it was the objectification of women. No way would Robbie want to be friends with a majorette!

Paris looked confused. "I mean, I guess you could look at it that way," she said. "But I don't. It's like stage makeup. On the football field, you're so far away that people can barely see you."

Tig waited for Paris to address the skimpy outfits, but she didn't. And strangely enough, Robbie let it slide right by. But Tig couldn't help imagining herself and Paris, side by side, in majorette uniforms. The contrast would be stark, to say the least.

It was all so weird. What could Robbie Chan possibly have in common with this majorette-wannabe who milked goats?

"What's say we run through 'It's Only Rock 'n Roll'?" Robbie said.

The girls had chosen this song because the Rolling Stones spanned so many generations of fans, it would be good for a set list to include something from them. Plus, their songs tended to have basic chord progressions that wouldn't be too tricky to learn. Robbie had suggested "It's Only Rock 'n Roll" with the idea that Paris could simply strum eighth notes while Robbie tackled the fast chord changes between A and G. Tig could handle the drums, but the bass was no picnic on this song, and she doubted Kyra would be able to handle it.

As Tig had feared, Kyra was all over the place. Before they even got to the first round of the chorus, she was lost.

"I take it you practiced this not at all?" Robbie asked.

"What makes you say that?" Kyra asked.

"Well, let's see. First of all, you're overplaying."

"What does that even mean?" asked Kyra. "Like, playing too well?"

"No, it means you're playing too many notes. You're supposed to be part of the rhythm section. The bass is a percussive instrument. And on this particular song, you have to play the melody because the guitar parts are mixed throughout the song, so the bass has to stay consistent to keep the core of the song anchored."

"Listen, Kyra," Tig said. "All you've got to do is plunk a few root notes. But when you're just that one beat off in the chorus, it gets me all turned around, and then the whole song's a train wreck."

"Chill out, y'all," Kyra said. "I had my teacher show it to me just last week. I haven't had a lot of time to perfect it, okay?"

"And have you practiced any on your own since your music lesson last week?" Tig asked.

"I've been busy," Kyra said.

Robbie let out a big sigh. "Paris, you did great," she said.

"Thanks," Paris replied. "Funny how the little bit I learned from those lessons in elementary school kind of came right back to me."

"Oh, sure, fawn all over the new girl to try to make me look bad," Kyra said.

"Nobody's trying to make you look bad, Kyra," Robbie snapped. "Trust me, you do a fine job of that all by yourself."

"Well, maybe if all I had to do was stand there and strum eighth notes while you did all the heavy lifting, you'd think I'd done a great job too," Kyra said.

"She has a point," Paris said. "What I was doing really wasn't that hard. Kyra, do you want to try it?"

"What do you mean?" Kyra asked.

"I'm just saying, if you want to swap, you can use my guitar, and I'll give it a try on the bass. I've always kind of thought the bass was cool."

Kyra looked at Tig as though this were some sort

of a trap. Tig shrugged. "Okay, fine," Kyra said. She handed Paris her bass, and Paris handed over her guitar.

"You just bought that guitar and already you're letting someone else use it?" Tig asked.

"It's rent-to-own," Paris said. "I figured, why sink a bunch of money into a guitar if this doesn't work out?"

"Good thinking," Tig said. She didn't add, *And with any luck, maybe it won't work out,* but she thought it.

"Can we take ten so I can show Paris the bass line?" Robbie asked.

"Sure," Tig said. "Anybody want to go in the house for some sweet tea?" They all did. "I'll bring some out for y'all," she said to Paris and Robbie.

When they got to the kitchen, Kyra launched in. "As if she's going to be able to teach Paris that bass line in ten minutes!"

"I know," Tig said. "That's kind of ambitious."

"Maybe she can," Claire said. "I thought it was nice of Paris to offer. Didn't you?"

"I think she's just trying to show off," Kyra said.

"The bass is a lot harder than it looks."

"Does anyone else find it weird that Paris and Robbie are friends?" Tig asked.

"Weird how?" Olivia asked.

"I mean, I just wouldn't have put the two of them together," Tig said. "What could they possibly have in common?"

"Summer camp?" Claire offered.

"An interest in music?" said Olivia.

Tig gave up. Obviously, they didn't see how mismatched Robbie and Paris were as friends. "Guess we'd better get back."

In the studio, Tig handed a glass of tea to Robbie and one to Paris. "How's it going?" Tig asked.

"Pretty good," Robbie said. "I think she can hang for the first stanza at least. But on this next run-through, everybody just keep going when the bass drops out."

"Agreed," Tig said.

Tig counted off and waited for the catastrophe. But it didn't happen. Paris was able to play the first several bars of the song, and when she couldn't play anymore, she stopped as the rest of the band continued. She'd played only a short portion of the bass line, but she'd played it accurately. Meanwhile, Kyra had flubbed the rhythm guitar eighth notes that were supposed to have been such a cinch.

"Told you Paris was a quick study," Robbie said after the song was over.

"Remember that time at camp when I had to tie that knot in, like, ten seconds?" Paris said. She and Robbie laughed. Tig felt completely left out. She resented that this newcomer—with her salon-perfect hair and swimsuit-model figure—had entered *her* studio, insinuated herself into *her* band, and was now having inside jokes with *her* cool friend.

They ran through the song twice more. Both times, Kyra messed up the rhythm guitar part, and Paris kind of nailed the bass line.

Much to Tig's dismay, it looked like Paris would be sticking around.

Chapter Ten

"**S**o?" Robbie asked Tig the next morning at school.

"So what?" Tig knew exactly *so what* but wanted to delay the inevitable as long as possible.

"So how great is Paris? I told you she was awesome."

"Yeah, she's nice," Tig said.

"What's the deal, Ripley?" Robbie said.

"What deal? There is no deal."

"Of course there is. You think I don't know you well enough to know when there's a deal?"

"It's fine," Tig said. "Your friend Paris is nice. What else do you want?"

"You don't like Paris!"

"I did not say that."

"You didn't *not* say it."

"I like her fine."

"Why don't you like her?"

"I just said I like her fine."

"Ripley."

"I mean, she's nice. I just . . . I don't know. She's not someone I would have pictured you being so attached to. She's just so different from you."

"She's not that different."

"Oh really?" Tig said. "Since when do you twirl a baton or milk goats?"

"Who cares? She's her own person. She's cool. Are we going to invite her to join the band?"

"She isn't exactly a seasoned musician," Tig replied.

"Neither were you when you started the band, and you've only been drumming for, like, a year. Paris doesn't exactly shred the ax, but she has some basic knowledge of guitar." Then she added, with a snide tone, "And she plays bass way better than your cousin after only ten minutes of instruction . . . so you know, there's that."

"Does every conversation have to circle back to Kyra?" Tig asked. "I know she's a problem. I'm keenly aware, okay?"

"I'm just saying, I don't think Paris is any more of a liability for Pandora's Box than Kyra is."

Tig sighed. "Probably not."

"Does that mean we can ask her to join?"

"I think we need to ask the other girls, don't you?"

"Sure, no problem. I don't mind asking them."

Tig hated the self-assuredness in Robbie's voice because she knew that Robbie was certain Olivia and Claire would be on board with her. What was worse, she knew that Robbie was most likely right.

"Fine. We'll bring it up at lunch."

"I look forward to it."

It wasn't exactly a fight, but it marked the first time Robbie and Tig had ever had a weird tension between them. Tig didn't like it. Robbie had always been the one person who got her, the one person who was always on the same page with her. Tig blamed Paris for this rift. But she also worried that if she continued to be negative about Paris, the rift with Robbie would only grow. As much as she disliked the idea of vying with Paris for the top spot on Robbie's friends list, she didn't want to lose Robbie as a friend altogether. Ugh. Of all the summer camps in the world, and of all the weeks to choose from each summer, why did Paris have to wind up at the same camp at the same time with Tig's coolest friend? And why did Robbie even like Paris anyway? That was the part that Tig still couldn't get her head around.

Later that day at the lunch table, Robbie wasted no time bringing up Paris to the other girls. "How much do you guys love Paris?" she asked.

"She's a doll," Olivia said.

"So sweet," Claire agreed. "I used my new soap this morning. Feel the back of my hand. It's like silk!" Everyone took turns touching Claire's indeed silky hand. Even Tig had no choice but to grudgingly agree that its softness rivaled that of a baby's butt.

"I think she'd be a great addition to the band," Robbie said. "What do you say?"

"Sure," Claire said.

"Sounds great," said Olivia.

Kyra and Tig said nothing. Everyone looked at them. "Kyra? Tig?" Robbie asked.

"It's Tig's band," Kyra said. "I think it should be her decision."

Tig was torn between being glad Kyra wasn't endorsing Paris and being mad that she left her to be the heavy. "I mean, she's great and all," Tig forced herself to say. "But she's a novice and we barely know her. That's all I'm saying."

"As I pointed out to Tig earlier," Robbie said, "Tig was a novice herself last year when she started the band. I say we give Paris a chance. Does anyone disagree with me?"

No one said anything.

"Then we have a consensus," Robbie said. "Tig, is

it okay with you if I give Paris the good news, or would you rather extend a personal invitation as the band's leader?"

Tig forced a smile. "Oh, I'll let you do the honors. Tell her we are all really excited to have her," she lied.

She hoped Robbie couldn't tell she was being fake.

"Hey, Tig," Will cut in. "I need to talk to you about Tuesday's tutoring."

"Sure, what about it?" Tig said, strangely relieved. She'd been dreading their next tutoring session, but at least someone had changed the subject from Paris.

"My mom has a meeting out of town that afternoon," Will said. "She wanted me to ask if your mom could drive me home after we finish."

"Oh yeah, okay," Tig said. "I'm sure that won't be a problem. I mean, it's the least I can do, for all your help with algebra and everything."

"So, Tig," Olivia said, "tell the truth."

Tig immediately turned red. "Tell the truth? Tell the truth about what? I don't know what you're talking about. I'm not hiding anything."

Olivia laughed. "Boy, are you ever on edge!" she said. "I guess your algebra grade really does have you rattled! All I was going to say was: tell the truth. . . . Is my boyfriend the best tutor ever, or what?"

Tig laughed nervously. "Oh," she said. "Right. I mean, yes. Will—your boyfriend—he's just the best."

Chapter Eleven

When Tuesday afternoon rolled back around, Tig found herself popping a mint before she went to the library. Then she inwardly chastised herself for having done so. *It doesn't matter if you have minty fresh breath because a) Will is not your boyfriend; he's Olivia's, and b) You're going to sit so far away from him that you could gnaw on some garlic and he'd never know it,* she told herself. And yet, somehow, her hands managed to find their way to her hair and fluff the roots before she went into the library and found Will at their table.

"Oh, hey!" Will said. His eyes sparkled so much

and his voice sounded so . . . not exactly surprised—
but maybe . . . unexpectedly pleased?—that it almost
felt like a chance meeting instead of a scheduled one.

Tig put her backpack onto the chair opposite
Will's.

"Why're you sitting over there?" Will asked.

"Why wouldn't I sit over here?"

"No reason. I just kind of thought, you know, it
might be easier to show you how to work problems
if you sat on the same side as me, so you could see my
paper and stuff."

"Oh," Tig said. "Right." That was *completely* logical.

When Tig sat down next to Will, he asked, "Do
you have any more mints?"

Tig blushed. So much for gnawing garlic. "Sure,"
she said, handing him the roll of wintergreen breath
mints.

"Ooh, I love these things," Will said. "My favorite
flavor."

"Mine too," Tig said.

"Did you know that if you sit in a dark closet and

bite down on one of these with your mouth kind of open, you can see sparks fly?" Will asked.

"No way!"

"It's true, I promise," he said. "I'll have to show you sometime." Then he blushed. "Not that we'd be, like, together in a dark closet, but . . ."

Tig couldn't help but laugh. "Yeah, I mean, it's not like you're a kidnapper or something." Will laughed too. Then Tig added, "And don't worry. I'm not going to even ask what you were doing sitting in a dark closet with a roll of wintergreen mints when you made this interesting discovery."

Will put his hand over his face. Then he said, "Don't you keep up with your Internet mythology? I had no choice but to try it."

They laughed a little bit more and then found themselves staring at each other in silence. Tig looked away and cleared her throat. "So, algebra . . . ," she said.

Tig allowed Will to teach her all about congruence, similarity, and transformations, even though she could have done the problems they worked in her sleep.

Playing dumb was excruciating for Tig; she hated being the damsel in distress. But it was her stupid lie about not understanding algebra that had gotten her into this mess in the first place, so she had to go along. She was relieved to get her mom's text message that she was waiting outside. "Time to go," said Tig.

"I appreciate your mom giving me a lift home," Will said.

"No problem," Tig said. Thank goodness the van was so roomy. Tig wasn't sure how much longer she could sit so close to Will and tell herself she felt nothing. As if the whole pretending not to understand algebra hadn't been torture enough.

When they got to the van, Tig's mom had about a dozen shoe boxes sitting on the front passenger seat. Behind that, her little brother and little sister were surrounded by equipment from their soccer team, and behind them were bags upon bags of groceries. "Sorry, you two, but you're going to have to crawl into the very back," Mrs. Ripley said. "After I drop Will off, I've got to get these two to practice, then drop you and the groceries at the house while I run these shoes to the repair shop to get rubber taps put on the heels." Mrs. Ripley let out a big breath and blew her bangs off her eyes.

First Tig, then Will, climbed into the very back two-seater bench. Will fastened his seat belt, but Tig couldn't get hers to work. "Mom," Tig said, "it's doing that thing again."

Mrs. Ripley sighed. "You know how that one sticks," she said. "You just have to give it a good jerk and then it will catch."

"I've given it a good jerk," Tig said. "It's busted."

"Will, could you help her out, please?" Mrs. Ripley said.

"Sure," Will said. He unfastened his seat belt and turned around to face Tig. Then he leaned over her, so close, they were almost touching, and began to tug on the top part of the seat belt that hung from the side of the van. "I think I almost got it," he said. "Almost." When he said the second *almost*, he made a sudden pulling movement, and his mouth brushed against

Tig's head. Even though her hair was covering it, and even though it was only for maybe a half second, she could feel Will's bottom lip ever so slightly skim the top of her ear. She immediately flushed.

"Got it," Will said.

"Oh, thank you, Will," said Mrs. Ripley.

"Yeah, thanks," said Tig.

Will smiled. He looked a little flushed himself. "My pleasure," he said.

Chapter Twelve

At the next practice, Paris once again brought her rent-to-own guitar. "I wasn't sure if y'all wanted me to do guitar or bass," she said. "So I practiced both parts."

The girls ran through "It's Only Rock 'n Roll" twice—the first time with Kyra on bass and Paris on guitar, and the second time with Kyra on guitar and Paris on bass. Paris messed up a couple of times on both instruments, but not as much as Kyra.

"I guess it's up to Kyra which one she wants to play," Tig said.

"Why's it up to Kyra?" asked Robbie.

"Seniority," Tig replied. "Kyra's been in the band longer."

"She certainly has," said Robbie. Her tone wasn't lost on Tig. Without saying the words, her voice said, *Kyra's been in the band a full year and still stinks, whereas Paris just started and is already better than she is. So why are we rewarding Kyra for never practicing?*

"I don't care either way," said Kyra.

That's exactly the problem, Tig thought. *She doesn't care. If she cared, she'd practice and we wouldn't even be having this conversation.*

"In that case," Robbie said, "I think we should let Paris choose."

"Well, if Kyra's sure she doesn't mind," Paris said.

"She just said she doesn't care," Robbie said. "So which instrument would you rather play on this song?"

"To be honest, I kind of enjoy the bass on this one," Paris said.

"Works for me," Robbie said. "Everybody okay

with that?"

The girls agreed this was fine with them, and the rest of the practice went off without much trouble, except for when Kyra flubbed her eighth notes on rhythm guitar.

Kyra was the last one left with Tig after all the other girls had been picked up from practice.

"You see what she just did, don't you?" Tig asked.

"What who just did?"

"Paris," Tig replied. "She just stole your instrument."

"She didn't steal my instrument," Kyra said. "I told her I didn't care if she played bass on this song."

"You really think that's all it's going to be—this one song? Kyra, how can you be so naïve?"

"What are you even talking about?"

"Don't you see? Little Miss If It's All Right with Kyra, I Just Love the Bass tricked you into swapping instruments with her!"

"I still don't see how it's a trick," Kyra said.

"How could you not see it? Don't tell me you're

taken in by her sugar-sweetness too? Mark my words: Paris knows exactly what she's doing. Don't you see it, Kyra? We don't have to have a rhythm guitarist, but we do have to have a bass player. She takes over on bass and it's hello, Paris, good-bye, Kyra."

"I hadn't thought of that," Kyra said. "Do you think Robbie put her up to it?"

The suggestion kicked Tig right in the stomach. She hadn't considered that Robbie might have been the mastermind behind it. But now that Kyra said it, of course it made perfect sense. "Do you think so?" Tig asked.

"I hadn't thought of it until now," Kyra said. "I didn't realize Paris was trying to take my place in the band, but now that you point it out . . . and it's no secret that Robbie's been wanting to get rid of me for some time. Do you think this was all Robbie's plan? Do you think she brought Paris in to replace me?"

Tig hated to think so, but it wasn't beyond the realm of possibility. Robbie had been growing increasingly frustrated with Kyra, and now that Kyra mentioned it, Paris's "coincidental" shift to the bass didn't seem so coincidental.

"Paris picked up that bass line in ten minutes last practice," Tig recalled. "Makes you wonder, doesn't it? Either Paris really is a quick study, or Robbie had already been teaching her the bass part beforehand."

Wow. Now that she'd said it out loud, Tig could hardly believe it. It was bad enough to think that Robbie liked Paris better than her, but the thought of Robbie conspiring with Paris to manipulate her way into the band almost made Tig sick.

Could the person Tig thought was her BFF actually be a snake in the grass?

"Call your folks and ask if you can stay for supper," Tig said. "Let's just hang out awhile." All the frustration Tig had felt toward Kyra the past several months seemed to fade away for the moment. Feeling betrayed by Robbie made Tig want to cling to her cousin. "We're not going to let them do this. Kyra, you're going to have to start kicking butt on the bass. You can't go down without a fight."

"Oh, trust me. I won't," Kyra said.

Tig felt reinvigorated. "We started this band, and we're going to show Paris and Robbie who's in charge around here."

Chapter Thirteen

It was awkward at school the next couple of days around Robbie. Tig tried to pretend that nothing was wrong, that she wasn't aware of what Robbie was up to. But Robbie could always tell when Tig was upset.

"What is with you lately?" Robbie asked at lunch.

"Nothing," Tig replied. "I don't know what you're talking about."

"For starters, you haven't made a joke in two days, and you always make jokes," Robbie said. "And you don't initiate conversation. When I talk to you, you answer, but it's like it's the bare minimum to be polite or something, not like you're really into it."

"I don't know," Tig said. "I certainly didn't realize I wasn't acting like myself."

"There it is again," said Robbie.

"What?"

"That weird formality in the way you talk. Since when do you say 'certainly'?"

Tig faked a laugh. "I think you're imagining things."

Robbie shrugged. "Whatever you say, Ripley."

It was a relief when the other girls got to the table. "Tig," Olivia said, "did you ask your mom if we could push practice back a half hour this Thursday? Coach says we won't get back till five."

"Yep," Tig said. "She was fine with it."

"That's actually better for me," Kyra said. "Mom's out of town, so Dad's going to have to leave work a little early to get me there."

"Is Paris going to make it?" Claire said to Robbie.

"Of course," Robbie replied. "She wouldn't miss it. She's completely amped about it." Robbie laughed. "See what I did there? Amped? Paris is amped? Get it?

Our bass player is amped."

Claire and Olivia laughed, so Tig and Kyra joined in, trying to sound genuine. Then Tig realized what she was laughing at.

"Did you just call Paris our bass player?" Tig asked. She tried to sound nonconfrontational, but she felt plenty confrontational.

"You know what I mean," Robbie said. "She's the bass player for the new song."

"Oh," said Tig coldly.

"Wait a minute," Robbie said. "Is that what this is all about?"

"What *what* is all about?" Tig said.

"That's why you've been acting so weird," Robbie said. "You're ticked that Paris's playing bass on 'It's Only Rock 'n Roll.'"

"I'm not ticked about anything," Tig lied. "I was just asking for clarification. That's all."

"You all were witnesses," Robbie said, gesturing to Olivia and Claire. "Kyra said she didn't care if Paris played bass on that song. Am I wrong?"

"That is what Kyra said," Olivia replied.

"Do you mind, Kyra?" Claire asked. "Were you just being polite?"

"It's fine," Kyra said.

"See, Ripley?" Robbie said. "Kyra said it's fine. Nobody's taking anybody's instrument, okay? Are we all cool?"

"Cool as the other side of the pillow," Tig said.

"Awesome," Robbie said. "Whew. That was starting to bug me."

"And you'll be glad to know that Kyra is determined to nail the rhythm guitar on the new song, so we should be humming right along come Thursday," said Tig.

"Is that right?" Robbie said. "So, Kyra, you've been logging the ol' practice hours, huh?"

"Totes," Kyra said.

"Heck, yeah," Robbie said. "I can hardly wait for Thursday!"

Tig agreed. And this time, she wasn't faking anything.

Chapter Fourteen

Tig may have been looking forward to the band's next practice, but she wasn't looking forward to that day's tutoring session with Will.

Or maybe she was. Which was the problem.

She kept telling herself she was dreading it. But if she hadn't been looking forward to spending that time with Will, alone in the library, then why had she spritzed perfume behind her ears that morning? And wondered when she did it if her gardeny smell would last all the way until after school? Most of the time, Tig never even wore perfume at all.

When she got to the library after school, Will wasn't there. Tig sat down at their usual table and took a deep breath. She thought about her perfume and whether it still lingered behind her ears, but since there was no way she could smell behind her own ears, she took a paper bookmark out of the novel she was reading and rubbed it back there a few times. Then she smelled the bookmark. Very faintly, she could still detect hints of pear and raspberry, plus some other scent she couldn't quite name. What was it? Sort of a musky, kind of . . .

"Why are you sniffing a bookmark?" Will said, standing behind her chair.

"What?" Tig said, jumping in her seat and quickly stuffing the bookmark back between the novel's pages.

Will pulled out the chair beside her. "I asked why you were sniffing a bookmark."

"I don't know what you're talking about," Tig said. "I was not sniffing a bookmark!"

Will laughed. "You were *so* sniffing a bookmark," he said. "Don't lie. I saw you!"

Tig blushed.

"It's okay," Will said. "I know why you were doing it."

"You do?" she asked.

"Well, I think I do, anyway," Will said. "Is it because you love the smell of books? Because I can totally relate. I've always loved the smell of books."

"Me too!" Tig said. And she really did. She was just so surprised that Will did too that she kind of forgot what had started the conversation in the first place.

"You know they have scented candles that smell like old books?" he asked. "My mom has one. She's where I get my weirdness from, I guess."

"Do they really?" Tig said. "That's cool!"

"But I do have one question," Will said. "If you like book smell, shouldn't you have been sniffing the book itself instead of the bookmark?"

"Oh," Tig said. That was a good point. "See, what I was doing . . . is . . . I wanted to see if the bookmark smelled like the book . . . you know, from having been in the book all that time."

"That makes sense," Will replied.

"Yes," Tig said. "Yes, it does." Thank goodness. It suddenly dawned on Tig that she'd just told another couple of lies. Was this becoming a habit with her now? Funny how one lie bred so many more. All this had started with her lie about a bad algebra grade, and now here she was, lying about sniffing a bookmark. Weird how that worked. *And I used to be a pretty decent, honest person,* Tig thought. *Didn't I?*

"How do you feel about area?" Will asked.

"I don't know," Tig said. "I guess I like it pretty well. It gets pretty crowded on McFarland Boulevard, though. That part kind of bugs me when my mom's trying to get me to drum lessons on time."

Will laughed. "I didn't mean how do you feel about *the* area; I meant how confident do you feel about area, as in measurement—area, surface area, volume?"

"Oh!" Tig said. "I knew that. I was just messing with you."

"Sure you were," Will said. They both grinned. While Will began showing Tig how to find the area of a rectangle—which of course she already knew how to do—Tig shivered. "You cold?" Will asked.

"Aren't you?" Tig replied. "What do they do in here, hang meat?"

"You want my hoodie?" Will unzipped his jacket and began taking it off.

"No, I couldn't," Tig said. "Then you'll be cold."

"I'll be fine," Will said. "Here. Take it." He placed the jacket around Tig's shoulders. She slid her arms inside and wrapped the soft cotton around her. It was still warm from his skin, and it smelled faintly like a walk in the woods on a fall day.

Tig took a deep breath. She drank in the scent and the warmth of the jacket.

And then she promised herself she'd find a way to end these tutoring sessions for good.

Chapter Fifteen

"**G**uess what," Tig said to Olivia at Thursday's practice.

"What?" Olivia asked.

"My algebra grade is back up," Tig said. "I've got a B in there right now." Of course, Tig had had a solid B all along, but Olivia didn't need to know that.

"That's awesome!" Olivia said. "Will really is a great tutor!"

"He must be," Tig said. "I think I've really turned a corner. It all makes sense now."

"Yay!" Olivia said.

"So Will's off the hook," Tig continued. "I won't

need any more tutoring."

Olivia said, "Tig, are you sure? If he's helped you this much, then maybe you should stick with it. It's obviously having an effect on you."

Oh, it's having an effect on me all right, Tig wanted to say. *But not the kind you want.*

"Nah," Tig said. "I'm golden. Besides, I can devote that time to practicing my drums!"

"If you say so," Olivia said. "But I'm sure Will wouldn't mind. . . ."

"Not necessary," Tig said. "So, that's settled. Tutoring's out; practice is in!"

Robbie jumped in. "Practice," she said. "Yes. I'm all for practice. Aren't you, Kyra?"

"Huh?" Kyra said.

"I said I'm all for practice," Robbie repeated. "How about you?"

"Sure," Kyra said. "Whatever."

But once they got started on the new song, it soon became apparent that Kyra had not been practicing any more than usual. Or maybe even at all.

Olivia and Tig carried their parts. Paris more than handled the bass, and Robbie and Claire both killed it.

Once again the weak link was Kyra.

"You took that to a whole 'nother level this time," Paris said to Robbie.

"I saw someone on the Internet say that open tuning makes anybody sound like Keith Richards," Robbie said. "I've been wanting to try it for a while but finally decided to go for it. I've tried it on a few songs now, tuning the third string down or sometimes an open D." As Robbie showed Paris what that meant, Claire and Olivia chatted with each other about their parts as well. Only Tig and Kyra were silent.

Tig's frustration sat in her stomach like a rock. Kyra had sworn to her that she'd practice, and now here they were, once again. Had Kyra really practiced like she'd promised? Was she just that bad a musician? Tig didn't know which to hope for. If it was just that Kyra wasn't practicing, it meant that she'd been lying about working harder, and that made Tig mad. If it was a genuine lack of talent, that meant that no matter what Kyra did, she was just lousy, and that made Tig sad.

"Overall, what did everybody think of that run-through?" Robbie asked.

"Well," Claire said, "I did feel like something was off somewhere. I'm not sure what."

Oh, you're sure, Tig thought. *We're all sure.* "Kyra, you're still having some trouble," Tig said. She might as well be the one to say it.

"I don't know what else y'all expect me to do," Kyra said.

"Play the song correctly?" Tig offered sarcastically. She almost felt bad after she'd said it. Maybe this really was the best Kyra could do. But Tig doubted it. She knew Kyra too well. Kyra probably hadn't followed through at all on her promise to practice more. She had never been much on follow-through with anything.

"Let me see if I can use an analogy that might be helpful," Robbie said to Kyra. "Let's say that the band is a body. And the lead guitar and the rhythm guitar are the hands. And this body, by the way, is right-handed, okay? So then the lead guitar is the right hand, doing most of the work, but the rhythm guitar is the left hand. And without the left hand, it's kind of hard for the right hand to accomplish much. If you tried to write something with your right hand, you'd still need your left hand to hold the paper in place. Do you get what I'm saying?"

"It's not that I don't know what the rhythm guitar is supposed to do," Kyra said. "It's just that it's a new instrument for me and I'm adjusting to it."

"You know what?" Robbie said. "You're totally right. It'll be better next week."

Tig was surprised that Robbie let Kyra off the hook so easily. Especially since Kyra's argument didn't hold a lot of weight, given that Paris was also playing a completely new instrument and seemed to have no trouble adjusting to it at all. Or since Kyra had had plenty of time to adjust to the bass but had still played it so poorly that Paris had taken over.

"Thanks, y'all," Kyra said. "I promise I'll have it by next practice."

After everyone else had left, Tig launched into Kyra yet again. "I thought we agreed that you were going to work harder!" she said.

"Calm down, Tig. We're just a middle-school girl band," Kyra said.

"And with that attitude, that's all we'll ever be," Tig replied. "Kyra, if we work hard, we could really do something with this band."

"Like what? Get a record deal?" Kyra laughed.

"That's exactly the kind of remark that makes me so frustrated with you," Tig said. "You're always talking about positive thinking, but that's only when there's no work involved. You can't just wish your way through life, waiting for things to happen for you. You have to make them happen. And the only way to make things happen is through hard work. Don't you get it?"

"Okay, okay, I get it. I'll practice more," Kyra said. But Tig could tell she so didn't get it, and the whiny tone in Kyra's voice made her even angrier.

"You'd better," Tig said. "Or you'll be out."

"Yeah, yeah," Kyra said. "You're always threatening

to kick me out of the band. You're not going to kick me out of the band."

"As I've already tried to explain to you, Paris is totally ready to pounce on your spot."

"You wouldn't dare. You can't stand Paris. You wouldn't give her my spot."

"Not if you start trying harder," Tig said. "But, Kyra, I can't do this for you. I can't want this for you. You have to want it for yourself and then do what needs to be done to get it."

"Yes, ma'am," Kyra said. Tig resented the implication that she sounded like a mother.

"As annoying as Paris is, I don't have to lecture her about pulling her weight," Tig said. "You'd better get your act together."

"I already said I would," Kyra said. "Sheesh! How many times do I have to promise?"

"Stop promising and start doing," Tig said. "Then you won't have to promise anymore."

Tig held out hope that maybe this time Kyra really would follow through.

But the next practice was no better. Tig's berating, begging, and encouraging hadn't made the least impression. Not even the suggestion that Paris was edging her out seemed to faze Kyra. She was still all over the place on each run-through of the song.

Kyra's dad picked her up at 5:35, which was slightly late. But even so, Kyra was the first to leave.

"Weird that all y'all's moms are late today," Tig said to the other girls after Kyra's car pulled away.

"It's actually not that weird," Robbie said. "I asked everyone to have their moms come at six today."

Tig's eyebrows knitted together. "Everyone except Kyra?"

"Everyone except Kyra," Robbie said.

Tig took a deep breath.

She knew what was coming. She had seen it coming for months, like a train in the distance.

And now that train was coming at her full speed, and there was no time to jump off the tracks.

Chapter Sixteen

"I don't suppose we have to explain why we called this meeting . . . ," Robbie began.

"Meeting?" said Tig. "Or ambush?"

"Please don't take it that way, Tig," said Claire. "You know we all love Kyra."

"Totally," said Olivia. "I mean, she's one of the most thoughtful people I know."

"That's true. Like when she gave us all a present for Saint Patrick's Day," Robbie said. "Those bags of green hard candies? Remember?" Tig remembered. That was so like Kyra. She loved giving gifts. If she could've figured out appropriate gifts for Presidents' Day and Martin Luther King Day, she probably would've done presents for those, too.

"And she's always the first person to call if she thinks you're upset," said Claire. "She's considerate; she's a good listener. . . ."

"She's always had my back," Tig said. "She always says we're the Bennett Mafia. She's never let anyone run me down if she's around to stop it." Tig felt guilty. Sure, Kyra could be super-annoying, but she'd always been there through thick and thin. How could Tig go along with this? Even if Kyra was bringing the whole band down?

"She's a great friend," Claire said.

"Just not a great bandmate," Tig said.

"If we're being honest, no, she's not," Olivia said. "Come on, Tig. You know we've all tried."

"I do know," Tig said. "And I appreciate it."

"Anyone else would've been gone a long time ago," Robbie said. "We've kept Kyra around all this time because she's your cousin and our friend."

"As long as we're being honest, Robbie," Tig said. "You know you kind of can't stand her."

"Look," said Robbie. "I know I've been harsh here and there. But honestly, it's not that I dislike Kyra as a person. She can be a lot of fun sometimes. It's just that I take my music very seriously, and it makes me angry when other people don't. I fully admit that."

"I hate to state the obvious," Tig said. "But y'all know Kyra doesn't exactly have a wide circle of friends. We're pretty much it. I mean, yeah, she likes telling people she's in a band . . . a *lot* . . . but I think she also likes being in a band with *us*. Even if she's terrible at music, the band makes her part of something."

"No one's saying we freeze her out," Robbie said. "She can still hang with us even if she's not in the band."

Tig sighed. "What do you think about all this, Paris?"

Paris put her hands up in a "don't shoot" gesture. "Hey, this is between y'all," she said. "It's only my third practice. And I ain't so hot a player myself yet."

"I just asked what you think," Tig said. "Can't you just give an opinion?"

Paris sighed. "I don't want to make anybody mad. Y'all've been real nice to me, and I know Kyra's your cousin, but from what I can tell about being in a band, you can't have a member who doesn't pull her weight. That dog just ain't gonna hunt."

"Dog?" Claire asked. "Hunt? Is this a colloquialism I'm not familiar with?"

"Yeah," Tig said. "It means it's not going to work."

"Oh," Claire said. "Charming."

Charming my foot, Tig thought. She was already irritated, and Paris's homespun sayings weren't helping. Seriously! How could Robbie stand her?

"So what do y'all want me to do?" Tig said. "As if I had to ask."

"You know what you have to do," Robbie said. "You've known for a long time, Tig. You just don't want to do it."

"Dang right she doesn't want to do it," Paris said. "Shoot, kicking your own cousin out of the band?

Kyra's gonna be madder'n a hornet. I don't blame Tig for not wanting to do it."

"But she *will* do it," Robbie said. "Won't you, Tig?"

Tig sat on the steps to the door of the studio and put her head in her hands. "Yes," she said. It pained her to say it. But Robbie and the rest of the girls were right. Tig had tried every way she could to make Kyra practice, but nothing had worked. She'd even directed her anger at Robbie and Paris because it had been too hard to face how angry she was with her cousin. Sure, she didn't like Paris, and maybe it had been Robbie's plan all along to replace Kyra with her. But could Tig really blame Robbie? Something had to be done, and Tig hadn't had the guts to do it. This had all been going on for far too long. "I'll do it. I'll tell her she's out of the band."

"Is there any way we can help?" Olivia asked.

"Do you want us to be there with you when you tell her?" said Claire.

"I don't know," Tig said. "I mean, on the one hand, if we were all there, it might seem less like it was all my doing. But on the other hand, I don't want her to feel ganged up on."

"You're right," Claire said. "But know this: we will all support you. When Kyra asks us about it, we won't put the blame on you and say we had no idea. We've all got your back. Right, girls?"

Everyone agreed.

"Why don't you sleep on it?" Robbie suggested.

"Sure," Tig said. "I bet I'll sleep like a baby tonight."

After the girls were picked up, Tig went inside.

"Late practice today," her mom said.

"Yeah," Tig said. "About that. . . ." She told her mom everything.

"Whoa," said her mother. "This is not good."

"Neither is Kyra's playing," Tig replied. "What am I supposed to do?"

Tig's mom called into the other room, "Dave, could you come in here for a second?" When her dad came into the room, Tig's mom gave him a brief update about the band situation. Then she said, "We can't keep it from her anymore. We've got to tell her."

"Tell me what?" Tig asked. "Y'all are scaring me."

"Let's have a seat," Mr. Ripley said. The younger kids were in the other part of the house, and the television was on. "They're occupied," he said to Tig's mom.

Tig couldn't stand it. "What's going on?"

"It's about your uncle Nick," said Mrs. Ripley.

"Uncle Nick? What about him? Is he okay?"

"He's fine," her mom said. "I mean, physically, he's fine."

"Then what?"

"Your aunt Laurie," Tig's dad said. "She's leaving him."

As Tig listened in shock, her parents told her the whole story. How Aunt Laurie didn't really have a sick friend out of town. How Uncle Nick had tried everything to save the marriage for Kyra's sake. How Aunt Laurie wouldn't change her mind.

"So that's what you two were talking about that day in the kitchen," Tig said. It was almost a relief to put the pieces together.

"Yes," said her mom. "We didn't want to tell you until we were certain they couldn't work things out. But now there's no chance of that."

No chance? Of course there was a chance! Why wouldn't there be a chance? Not that Tig had ever really liked Aunt Laurie, but she was Kyra's mother. And Uncle Nick's wife. And *they* loved her. They were a family. Didn't that mean anything?

"Maybe they just need a vacation or something," Tig said. "Maybe Uncle Nick could send her roses? She likes stuff like that."

Tig's parents looked at each other. "Believe me, Tig," her mother said. "Uncle Nick has tried everything he could. It's over."

"No," Tig said. "I'm sure they'll work it out. Kyra can't do that every-other-weekend thing that kids with divorced parents have to do. Nobody in our family has ever been divorced! They have to fix it!"

"Tig," her mom said, "there are things that you're just too young to understand. The marriage cannot be fixed. Please just take my word for it and let it go."

"How can I just let it go? How can any of us? This is awful! Does Kyra know?"

"They're telling her tonight," Tig's dad said.

"Oh, poor Kyra!" Tig said. "Now I feel really awful about the band. Do you think this is why she's been so terrible at the bass?"

"I don't know, honey," said her mom. "Maybe she's been distracted. Maybe she's just not musically inclined. It's hard to say."

"Maybe you and your friends could give her a little more time," Tig's dad said. "These next few months are going to be tough for your cousin."

Tig nodded. "I'm sure when the girls find out about the divorce, they'll cut her some slack."

A few hours later Tig's mom's phone rang. "Of course," Tig heard her mother say.

Shortly after that, Kyra walked in the door. Her face was red and puffy. Tig was almost afraid to speak, to move. She didn't know what she should say or do. But when Kyra's cracking voice said, "Oh, Tig!" and she started to cry, Tig instinctively ran to her cousin and pulled her into a tight hug. They held the embrace for some time, sobbing together.

"You're going to be okay," Tig kept saying over and over. "You're going to be okay."

Chapter Seventeen

"I just don't understand," Kyra told Tig as they lay in bed that night. "I know Dad still loves Mom. I even asked him outright. I said, 'Do you still love Mom?' "

"What did he say?"

"Nothing. He just looked away and started crying. Then Mom said that I needed to stop. So I asked her point-blank, 'Do you still love Dad?' "

"And what did she say?"

"She said no," Kyra said. "It was so . . . I don't know. . . . Like it was nothing. Like I'd just asked if she wanted sausage on her pizza."

Tig almost laughed. She'd never seen Aunt Laurie eat a slice of pizza in her life, and if she did, Tig was sure it would have been on a whole grain pita with low-fat cheese and some sprinkling of wheat germ or something. Aunt Laurie would never have risked her thighs to sausage pizza.

"What did your parents tell you?" Kyra asked. "Did they tell you the reason?"

"No," Tig replied. "They said I was too young to understand. That it was an adult thing."

"That's such a cop-out," Kyra said. "Look, people don't just fall out of love and decide to tear their family apart, do they? There's got to be a reason."

"I don't know," Tig said. "Adults are weird, Kyra. They don't make any sense."

"That's the part that kills me," Kyra said. "I need it to make sense. At least then, if I could understand, I could deal. But this whole 'Poof! It's over!' stuff . . . I just can't."

"Just know I'm here for you, Kyra. And our friends will be too. They'll be so sorry to hear about this."

"No!" Kyra sat up in bed. "You can't tell them!"

"What? Why not?"

"It's too humiliating!" Kyra said. "No one can know!"

"How is this humiliating?" Tig asked. "You didn't do anything. These things just happen. Take Will, for instance. His folks divorced when he was little. Lots of people at school have divorced parents. Olivia's dad is her stepdad. Her real dad moved away when she was a baby. You know that."

"That's fine for Will and Olivia and whoever else," Kyra said. "But this is me. These are *my* parents. And I'm sure that when they realize what a huge mistake this is, they're going to get back together. And when they do, I don't want everyone talking for the rest of my life about how they almost got divorced."

"Kyra, it doesn't sound like they're going to get back together. My mom said it was over and there was no saving it."

"No offense, Tig, but Aunt Julie doesn't know everything."

Tig didn't even try to defend her mom. Part of her hoped Kyra was right. And the other part of her was just glad to see Kyra riled a little bit. Because at least when she was riled, she wasn't crying and heartbroken.

"Promise you won't tell anyone?" Kyra asked.

"I promise," Tig said.

Chapter Eighteen

Without giving them any reason, Tig somehow managed to convince Robbie and the others to give Kyra more time.

"How much more time?" Robbie had asked.

"A month?" Tig had proposed.

But she'd been able to get only a two-week reprieve. The girls were firm. If only they'd known what was going on, Tig felt sure they wouldn't have been so resolute. But of course, she'd promised Kyra she wouldn't tell them, so two weeks it was.

Naturally, in those two weeks, Kyra played worse

than ever.

Tig went to her mom for advice. "I never should've asked Kyra to be in the band in the first place," she said. "I knew she wouldn't stick with it. Kyra never sticks with anything."

"Mixing family and business is a tough one," said Mrs. Ripley. "Remember that time I paid my cousin Russell to put in our new kitchen cabinets? Aunt Coila was all, 'Oh, Russell's so handy and he'll do an extra good job for you and he really needs the money.' So against my better judgment, I hired Russell to do the work, and you see what I got." She opened a cabinet door and closed it, but it didn't shut all the way. "But what can you do? Can't sue him. He's family."

"But would you hire him again?" Tig asked.

"Not by a long shot," said her mom.

"So what am I supposed to do? Let Kyra just keep on making cabinets that don't shut?"

"Oh, sweetie. I wish Kyra would let the other girls know what's going on."

"She won't, though. And she's sworn me to secrecy.

She's convinced that Uncle Nick and Aunt Laurie are going to work it out."

Mrs. Ripley shook her head. "The poor child."

"And I can't tell Kyra the other girls want her out of the band, because it will hurt her feelings, and she can't handle any hurt feelings right now. And besides, then I'd be going behind their backs. It's a no-win situation."

"I'm sure you'll figure something out," said Mrs. Ripley.

Well, her mom had no answers. So Tig decided to turn to the one place that always had all the answers.

Chapter Nineteen

When Tig typed *how to kick someone out of your*, the search engine offered to finish the statement with the word *house* but not *band*. But when Tig went ahead and finished typing the entire statement, there were nearly thirty-one million results.

Well, at least she wasn't the first person to have this problem.

Just to delay things, she typed, *how to kick your cousin out of your*, and the search engine once again offered *house*. When Tig finished the whole statement, there were nearly two million hits, but none of them dealt with the actual problem, just contained the words somewhere.

So maybe Tig *was* the first person to have to kick her cousin out of a band.

There was actually some pretty good advice on a few musician websites about how to get rid of a band member. Tig read for about half an hour, and it seemed the consensus was to be up-front and honest about the whole thing. But there was no *unless the band member's parents are also getting a divorce and he/she is in denial about it.* But honesty was supposed to be the best policy, wasn't it? And if Tig didn't tell Kyra herself, and tell her gently, there was bound to be a mutiny at the next practice. Robbie would blow up and say something harsh. That would be way worse.

So Tig decided she'd rather be up-front and honest with Kyra herself.

But maybe over the phone. And to delay the confrontation, she thought maybe it could wait until tomorrow night.

Just as Tig had been awkward around Robbie a few

weeks before, the next day she was awkward around Kyra at school. Kyra, though, was oblivious. Maybe she was so preoccupied with the divorce, she wasn't even thinking about the band. Or maybe she knew she was in danger of being kicked out of the band but didn't want to know. Either way, she didn't challenge Tig on her behavior and seemed completely normal at the lunch table that day.

"Let me guess," Robbie whispered to Tig. "You haven't told her yet."

"I'm going to do it tonight," Tig said. "Over the phone. That way, she can be upset in private for a while."

Tig followed through and called Kyra after supper that evening. "I need to talk to you about the band," she said.

"You and that band," Kyra said. "Don't you ever want to talk about anything else? I'm so sick of the band all the time."

"Well, maybe that's good," Tig said. *Up-front and honest,* Tig reminded herself.

"What's that supposed to mean?"

"Kyra, you know you haven't been pulling your weight. Not for a long time. And the other girls don't know your situation, and you won't let me tell them, so they can't be very understanding about something they don't even know about, and . . ."

"So you're kicking me out of the band?" Kyra laughed. "Yeah, right." There was a pause. "You're not laughing," Kyra said.

"No, I'm not laughing because I'm serious," Tig said. "Kyra, I don't want to hurt you. I know this is a difficult time for you."

"Tig, come on," Kyra said. "If you're trying to get my attention, then fine. You've got it. I'll practice more."

"Come on, Kyra. We've already been down that road," Tig said. "Just think of it as a nice long break. You just said you're sick of the band. Now you won't have to worry about it anymore. You'll have plenty of time to focus on feeling better, and then maybe you can come back when things have calmed down and you can give it more effort."

"This is coming from Robbie, isn't it?" Kyra said. "Oh, that's just perfect. One minute you're all 'it's our band and Robbie can't push us around,' and the next, you're doing whatever she wants! Well, Olivia and Claire won't go along with it."

"Kyra, they already have," Tig said as gently as possible.

"*What?*" Kyra said. "So you've all been conspiring against me behind my back, huh?"

"Of course not."

"Well, you must've discussed it sometime, and I certainly wasn't there for it, so I'd call that going behind my back! How could y'all treat me like this?"

"We didn't conspire, we aren't ganging up on you, and we're not trying to treat you unfairly. You know this is nothing personal," Tig said. "We all love you to death, Kyra. It's just that the band thing isn't working out for you. We all still want to be your friends."

"Friends don't treat friends like this!" Kyra said. "And neither do cousins! How could you? Wait until my mom hears about this! And then you can be sure she'll call your mom, and then your mom will kill you!"

"I don't think so," Tig said.

"You mean Aunt Julie knew about this?"

"I mentioned it to Mom, yes."

"And she's letting you do this to me?"

"Come on. Be fair. No one is doing anything to you. It's just not working out. It's been a long time coming, and you know it."

Seeing that anger was getting her nowhere, Kyra switched to pouting. "I think you're mean," she said.

"Kyra, you know I'm not trying to be mean! You know I love you! And the other girls do too. If you'd just let me tell them about the divorce—"

"No!" Kyra shouted. "I keep telling you, there isn't going to be any divorce! Why do you keep trying to gossip about my family to the band?"

"That's not fair," Tig said. "You know that's not what's happening. Kyra, please—"

"You think this is over, but it's not," Kyra said. "You're not going to get away with this."

"Please, calm down. It's going to be all right."

"Oh, trust me. I'm calm. I'm seeing things very clearly now. And soon so will everyone else!"

"Kyra . . ."

But all Tig heard on the other end was silence. Kyra had hung up on her.

Chapter Twenty

"**A**nybody seen or talked to Kyra yet this morning?" Tig asked when she joined her friends in the gym before school. She'd filled them in last night via text that she'd given Kyra the boot and that it hadn't gone well. At all. But of course, she'd kept her promise and hadn't told them about the divorce.

"Talked to? No," Robbie said. "Seen? Yes."

"Uh-oh," said Tig.

"Yeah," said Robbie.

"We said hi to her this morning, but she just walked right past us," Olivia said.

"Wouldn't even look at us," added Claire. "She acted like we didn't exist."

Tig sighed. "She'll have to forgive us eventually. Everybody else is already cliqued up for the year. There's nowhere for her to go, right?"

"Not exactly," said Robbie. She nodded toward the place in the gym where the popular girls sat.

Tig looked. "Oh no," she said. "Kyra's trying to sit in the Bot Spot?"

"*Trying* is the operative word, obvs," said Robbie. Kyra was tentatively perched on the end of a bleacher, one hip on and one hip off. She seemed to be working extra hard to steady herself so as not to fall. None of the popular girls were looking at Kyra or talking to her. It was clear to anyone observing that Kyra was not an invited guest but an interloper.

"Why does she keep trying to join the Bots?" Tig said. "Doesn't she see that they don't want her? Why does she keep humiliating herself?"

"I suppose she thought this might be an opportunity," Robbie said.

"An opportunity? How?" Tig asked.

"Let's see . . . last year, when we kicked Haley out of the band as lead singer, she and the other Bots did everything they could to destroy us. Or have you forgotten all that unpleasantness?"

Tig absolutely had not forgotten. The Bots had been vicious in their attempts to drag her reputation through the mud and put her on the level of pond scum in the social hierarchy. "Of course I remember," Tig said. "But it's weird. Regan's in my math class, and she's been pretty human to me so far this year."

"Three words," said Robbie. *"It's. A. Trap!"*

"My thoughts exactly," said Tig. "I just can't figure out her game."

"But you can be sure there is one," Robbie said.

"I've hardly had time to give Regan a passing thought in the last few weeks, what with worrying about Kyra." Then Tig quickly added, "And the band, I mean."

"I'm still waiting for one of you to explain how kicking Kyra out of the band is an opportunity for her to become a Bot," said Olivia. "What's she going to say, 'I stink at the bass so don't you want to be my friend'?"

"More like, 'Oh, Haley, we have so much in common because mean old Tig kicked me out of her stupid band too,' " said Robbie.

"Oh," Olivia said. "Gotcha."

"It doesn't appear to be working," Claire said. "Is it just me, or are they going out of their way to freeze her out?"

The girls watched the scene playing out in the Bot Spot. The back of the popular girl right next to Kyra seemed to be inching closer to her. Now only about a third of Kyra's butt was still on the seat. And the Bots still weren't looking at or talking to her.

Tig's heart couldn't help but go out to Kyra, in spite of the way she'd acted last night. First her parents, then the band, now this fresh embarrassment. Poor Kyra. "This is unfortunate," Tig said. "Just very, very unfortunate."

"What's unfortunate?" asked Will as he and his friend LaDarius walked up to the girls. "You mean

Kyra over at the Bot Spot, looking desperate?"

"You noticed too?" Olivia said, making room for the boys to sit.

"Girl drama in a gymnasium," LaDarius said. "It's hard to miss."

"I hate girl drama," said Olivia.

"It's really ridiculous," Will said. "At least with guys, we know where we stand. A wedgie here and there or they 'accidentally' slam you in PE or sports practice, and then everybody gets on with real life."

"Oh, is that why you always get owned in PE?" LaDarius said. "And here all this time, I thought it was because you stink."

Will shoved LaDarius, who laughed.

"Will's right, though," LaDarius continued. "Girls just take it to an extreme. If one girl hates another girl, she's got to make all her friends hate her too. It must be exhausting."

"Pretty much," said Tig.

"I guess it's funny, in a sad way," said Claire.

"What?" asked Tig.

"We finally solve the problem of Kyra and the bass, and now we've got a new Kyra problem altogether."

The girls nodded. The two boys were no longer listening, though. They had already lost interest in the whole thing and were discussing a video game. Tig couldn't help but envy them. Boys' friendships seemed so much easier.

"How do we solve this one?" Robbie asked.

"I was hoping," Tig said, "that you could tell me."

Chapter Twenty-One

"What gives with your cousin?" Regan asked before algebra started.

"What do you mean?" said Tig.

"Don't play dumb," Regan said. "You saw her sitting in our part of the gym this morning."

"Yeah. So?"

"So what's she trying to pull?"

Tig didn't know how to respond. She thought back to Robbie's *"It's. A. Trap!"* comment before school. "You should probably ask Kyra that question, not me."

"I have to hand it to you," Regan said. "You're

pretty loyal."

Tig looked at her, confused.

"Just saying, Kyra didn't seem to have any qualms about throwing *you* under the bus."

"Under what bus? What did she do?"

"It was all pretty tiresome, really. She came up to Haley and me this morning and said that if we still wanted to take down your band, she'd help us."

"What?!" Tig could hardly believe it. Maybe, she thought, she shouldn't believe it. After all, this information was coming from Regan.

"Yeah," said Regan. "She was all, 'Tig kicked me out of the band and poor, pitiful me' and 'Anything you want to know about the band, I can tell you.' "

"That little sneak!" Tig wished she hadn't said it out loud. Perhaps this really was a trap and she was walking right into it.

"That's pretty much what we all thought too," Regan said.

"What did you say to her?"

"We told her thanks but no thanks," said Regan.

"Why?" *Exactly what was Regan's angle here?*

"Because," said Regan, "just like I told Kyra, destroying your band is so last year. That's all ancient history now."

"Is it?" Tig asked. "How come?"

"It was all pretty stupid to begin with, don't you think?" said Regan. "So childish. And besides, y'all were pretty good in that video—that fake ad thing."

"The spot we did for the university's student project," Tig said.

"Yeah. It wasn't half bad."

"Thanks," said Tig. The idea that this was a trap kept rattling around inside Tig's head, but she couldn't figure out how Regan's refusal to help in Kyra's revenge plot— or Regan's complimenting the band's video—could entrap anyone. Maybe Regan was just that good: maybe she'd gone from overt meanness last year to schemes so diabolical that Tig couldn't even fathom them.

"What do you think Kyra will do now?" Tig asked.

"I don't know," Regan said. "But you'd think she'd have bigger fish to fry than your band, what with her parents getting a divorce and all."

"Kyra told you about that?"

"Please. She didn't have to. Everybody in town knows."

Tig shook her head. "Kyra's going to freak."

"Well," Regan said, "it's really not that bad. Both of my parents have been married a few times. You just learn to roll with it."

"It's kind of a big deal to us," Tig replied.

"Hey, if it makes you feel any better, my mom and all her friends think Kyra's mom is nuts to leave her dad. They think your uncle's great and also kind of a hottie."

Tig didn't know whether to be grossed out or feel a sense of family pride. "Thanks," she said. "I appreciate that. I think. And also, I appreciate—you know—the fact that you're not trying to kill my band anymore."

"No problem. As far as I'm concerned, you and I are cool," Regan said.

Tig nodded, then turned around in her seat and opened her algebra book.

She was so stunned that her aunt and uncle's divorce was already news around the school that she could hardly think straight. In fact, she didn't even realize she was staring at Will from the time he walked in the door until the time he sat down. Somehow, examining his high cheekbones and the symmetry of his eyebrows soothed her frazzled nerves. She couldn't take her eyes off him.

"Is there something on my face?" Will said, rubbing his cheek.

"No," Tig said, snapping out of her haze. "Sorry. I've just got the stares. Lost in thought. There's nothing on your face."

Except lots and lots of good-looking, Tig thought.

Chapter Twenty-Two

Tig wondered where Kyra would sit at lunch that day, since she refused to even speak to any of the Pandora's Box girls. And, of course, Tig knew from her conversation with Regan that the Bots table wouldn't be an option. So what would Kyra's next move be?

It turned out that Kyra managed to find an empty seat at the Scholars' Bowl table. If the brainiacs noticed Kyra sitting with them, they didn't seem to mind. They just kept taking turns asking one another questions from trivia apps.

"I tried to wave Kyra over here, but she wouldn't

look at me," Olivia said.

"Maybe I should go get her," Claire said, "and ask her to come back to our table."

"No," Tig said. She couldn't face Kyra right then; she had no idea what to say to her. First of all, Tig had no idea if Kyra knew that everyone in town was talking about the divorce. If she didn't, Tig didn't want to be the one to tell her. Plus, there was the whole attempted betrayal of the band to the Bots. Both of these things together were just too much to think about all at once. "Let Kyra sit with the geniuses a few days," said Tig.

"You sound mad," Robbie said. "What did she do now?"

Tig wondered if she should even say anything. But she wasn't very good at hiding her feelings, and it was obvious she was mad about something. She couldn't tell them about the divorce; she'd promised Kyra she wouldn't say a word about it—even if it *was* just a matter of time until they heard it from someone else. Tig decided the only way to explain her anger was to tell them about what Kyra had said to Regan that morning. Plus, she decided, when it came down to it, maybe it would be best if the other girls were on guard against any other attacks Kyra might try. "She offered to help the Bots destroy our band."

"She what?" Robbie said. "And you know this how?"

"Because Regan told me all about it in algebra."

"Regan," said Robbie, as though she needed to make sure she'd understood Tig correctly. "And you believe Regan?"

"Actually, I do," said Tig. "What would she have to gain by telling me?"

"I'm not sure," said Robbie. "But I wouldn't trust Regan. There must be something to gain. Otherwise she wouldn't do it. Regan always has an angle."

Tig nodded, but she wasn't sure she agreed. Maybe this time Regan didn't have an angle. Maybe, like Regan had said, last year's feud was childish and all behind them. Maybe the two of them really were cool now.

But just in case, Tig decided she'd remain wary of Regan.

In the meantime, she still wasn't sure what to do about Kyra. Maybe, given the family crisis, she should just forget what Kyra had done and try reaching out to her again.

But the sting of the betrayal was still sharp, and Tig couldn't just let it go. Not yet, anyway. Tig tossed it around in her mind the rest of the day until she finally made a decision:

When Kyra was ready, Kyra would have to come to her.

Chapter Twenty-Three

"I've got to hand it to her," Tig said that Friday morning in the gym. "I didn't think she could keep it up this long." Robbie, Claire, Olivia, and Will looked at the Human Google section of the bleachers. While none of the Scholars' Bowl kids seemed to be actively engaging with Kyra, they were giving her full access to their seating space, rather than crowding her out the way the Bots had.

"Maybe she's found her new crowd," said Will.

"I can't believe she hasn't spoken to us in three whole days," Claire said. "This is crazy! She won't even reply to my texts."

"I called a couple of times, but she won't answer," Olivia said. "I'm worried about her. Tig, did you know there's a rumor going around . . . I hate to ask, but . . . somebody told my mom yesterday that Mr. and Mrs. Bennett are getting a divorce."

"Whoa!" said Robbie. "Is that true, Tig?"

Tig didn't know how to respond. She'd promised Kyra, after all, that she wouldn't tell the other girls. But maybe now that it was the talk of the town, and now that Kyra had cut ties with them all, that promise was nullified.

"Yeah," Tig said.

"Well, that explains a lot," Robbie said. "Man, why didn't you tell us? I wouldn't have insisted we cut her loose at a time like this!"

"She swore me to secrecy," Tig said. "She said she was embarrassed. I couldn't say anything. But that's why I kept trying to get y'all to give her another chance."

"I wish we'd known," said Claire.

"Yeah," said Olivia. "I feel kind of petty, worrying about the band, when Kyra's whole family is falling apart. Oh, Tig! What can we do? Kyra needs us! And I miss her. Don't you?"

"Nah," Tig said. "It's no big deal."

"Nobody's buying it, Ripley," said Robbie. "Of course you miss her. She's your cousin."

"I know she is," Tig said. "And I do hate it about the divorce. For her and for my uncle Nick. But none of that changes the fact that Kyra betrayed me."

"The sad thing is, that's probably the way Kyra feels about you," Olivia said. "She thinks you mistreated her, and it hurts even more because you're family. Not that she isn't mad at us, too, but she probably expected you to stick up for her more because of what's happening with her folks right now. I know Kyra's out of line about the band, but we've got to remember she's going through a lot right now."

"You ought to be a shrink," Robbie said.

"I'm just trying to give Kyra the benefit of the doubt," Olivia said. "We need to understand where she's coming from, cut her some slack."

"You're right. You know, Tig, it is the first Friday of the month," Robbie said.

"I'd almost forgotten," she replied.

The band had developed kind of a standing monthly slumber party the first Friday night of every month at Tig's house. They'd practice some, but mostly it was just fun.

"Are we still on?" Claire asked.

"Of course," said Tig.

"Maybe we could ask Kyra to come," Olivia said.

"Or is that salt in the wound?" Robbie asked. "Like, 'Hey, come to the band slumber party for the band we kicked you out of'?"

"I think we should try to include her," Claire said. "If she'll let us."

"You're right," said Tig. "I'm still kind of mad about the Bots thing, but in the end, I guess there was no harm done. We could show Kyra that we still care about her even though she tried to stab us in the back."

"And maybe we could just skip practice at this

one," Claire said. "Just try to be there for Kyra."

"Good idea," said Tig.

"Great," said Robbie. "I'll let Paris know. I'd mentioned it to her but kind of had her on standby until it was confirmed."

"Oh, good," said Tig. *Great,* she thought. *Now Paris's spending the night at my house?* Wasn't it enough that she had to put up with her being in the band at all?

"I'll call Kyra after school," Tig said. "If she won't pick up, I'll call Uncle Nick and have him tell her she's invited. She can't stay mad forever."

Chapter Twenty-Four

The slumber party started at four that afternoon. Tig had tried to call Kyra, but as predicted, she'd let the call go to voicemail, so Tig had called Uncle Nick. He sounded like a wreck, but he put Tig on hold while he asked Kyra about the sleepover. He'd clicked back over to Tig after only a minute or so and told her that Kyra didn't feel up to coming to the party.

Since Kyra would be a no-show, the girls saw no harm in getting in their practice time.

Robbie was plugging in her amp when Olivia announced, "Paris's here." Robbie and Claire went to the door of the studio to greet her. Tig hung back and pretended to fiddle with the tension on her foot pedal.

"Check it out, ladies," Paris said when she got inside the studio. She unzipped a black cloth case and revealed a black-and-white bass.

"It's like an Oreo cookie," said Robbie. "Suh-weet!"

"It's not entirely black, though," Paris said. She tilted the instrument back and forth so the light hit it in different ways.

"Aaah!" Robbie said. "It's electric blue in the center of the black! I love it!"

"Yeah, me too," said Paris. "I figured it would look really cool under stage lights when we play gigs."

"Did you rent it from the music store?" Tig asked.

"No," said Paris. "Bought it off eBay. Can you believe only ninety bucks for the bass, the amp cord, and the gig bag? And free shipping, too. Total score."

"Oh," said Tig. "So you bought it outright. I thought you were just playing bass for the one song."

"I mean, well, I just thought, you know, since Kyra... I mean, I thought since we didn't have a bass player..."

"It's fine," Tig said. "Just trying to stay up-to-date on what's happening with the band. That's all."

"Ripley, it's okay for Paris to play bass, isn't it?" asked Robbie.

"Of course. Why wouldn't it be?" Tig replied.

"You tell me," said Robbie.

There it was again . . . that tension that had never existed between Tig and Robbie before Paris had come along.

"I just said it's fine," said Tig. "Let's practice."

They ran through "It's Only Rock 'n Roll" twice before stopping. It was markedly better than they'd ever played it before because they no longer had Kyra flubbing notes on the bass or the rhythm guitar.

"That was good," Tig said. "Let's do it once more."

The third time was the best yet. The girls were so absorbed in their instruments that it took a few seconds before they noticed that Claire had stopped singing.

Then, one by one, each girl stopped playing, and their unexpected audience slowly began clapping.

"Bravo," said Kyra. "Bravo."

Chapter Twenty-Five

"**W**hat?" Kyra said. "Isn't anyone going to say anything?"

"Kyra, we thought you weren't coming," Tig said.

"I changed my mind," she said.

"Okay," Tig said.

"I guess you decided that kicking me out wasn't enough, huh?" Kyra said. "Y'all wanted me to come and see how great the band is without me?"

"Of course not," Tig said. "You know we wouldn't do that. We were trying to offer an olive branch. You haven't spoken to any of us all week."

"Oh, that," said Kyra. "Was that rude of me?" Her tone was sharp. It was obvious that she felt very much in control of whatever this situation was.

"I don't know," Tig said, equally calm. "What do you think?"

"I think," said Kyra, "that maybe I was too hasty in deciding not to talk to all of you. I think maybe I have quite a bit to say after all."

Olivia didn't seem aware of any irony or venom from Kyra. She replied, "We know you were hurt, Kyra. It wasn't our intention to hurt you."

"Isn't that a shame?" Kyra said. "Because I think hurt should always be intentional. Like right now, for instance."

"Come on, Kyra," Robbie said. "We all want to be here for you. We know you're having a tough time. We're all really sorry about your folks."

Kyra turned sharply to Tig. "You told them?"

"No," said Tig. "I mean, yes . . . but—"

"I knew I couldn't trust you! First the band and now this!"

"Kyra," Robbie said. "You've got this all wrong—"

"Is that so, Miss Chan?" said Kyra. "Because I think you're the one who's got a few things wrong. But I'm about to set you straight."

"Kyra, what are you trying to do?" said Tig.

"I just thought that your best friend, Robbie, should know how you feel about her other best friend Paris."

"Kyra . . . ," said Tig.

"Robbie, I'm sure you'll find it very interesting to learn that Tig hates Paris's guts."

"Kyra!" Tig said. She couldn't think of anything else to say. She was too shocked.

"Yes, just being around her sets Tig's teeth on edge. Furthermore," Kyra continued, "she thinks that you planned all along for Paris to steal the bass from me. That's why she kept nagging me to practice. She said it was time someone showed you who's boss."

"That's not what I said!" Tig said. "You're twisting my words!"

"Then just what did you say, Ripley?" asked Robbie.

"Don't you see what she's trying to do? She's trying to get revenge by turning us against each other!"

"So far it's working," said Robbie.

"Go ahead and deny it," said Kyra. "Tell them I'm lying about how you can't stand Paris."

Everyone looked at Tig.

"I may have said something to that effect," Tig admitted. The girls gasped.

"And you thought I engineered this whole thing with Paris playing the bass?" Robbie said. "Don't you know me better than that? It was just the way things played out. I didn't plan any of it!"

"I'm sorry," said Tig.

"Sorry only goes so far," said Robbie.

"Kyra!" Uncle Nick called from the driveway. "Let's roll!"

"Wish I could stay longer," Kyra said. "But you girls have a *great* time."

When Kyra was gone, the girls stared at Tig.

"I can explain," she said.

Chapter Twenty-Six

It was a good thing the girls were spending the night at Tig's and had no means of a fast getaway; otherwise, they might not have agreed to hear her out.

They all went inside and sat on the floor and on the bed in Tig's room. The tension was palpable as they waited for Tig to explain herself.

Tig took a deep breath before she began. "First, I need to say that I'm sincerely sorry."

"Then you did say those things," Robbie said.

"Yes," Tig said. Sure, for a second she'd considered denying everything and saying that Kyra was lying.

But she knew from the lies she'd told to cover her true feelings for Will that lies could easily turn into a spark that starts an inferno. She also knew that if she got caught, everything would just be ten times worse.

"I thought maybe Kyra was lying," Claire said. "I can't decide which is worse—Kyra lying or you saying such awful things. Tig, why would you do something like that?"

"Because . . . ," Tig said. She looked down. "Because I was jealous, okay? I admit it. I was jealous."

"Jealous of what?" Paris asked.

"Of everything!" Tig replied. "I mean, look at you! Do you own a mirror? You're all, like, perfect and stuff, and to top it off, you just took to the bass like a duck takes to water, and . . . well . . . most of all, I was jealous of your friendship with Robbie."

"Why would you be jealous of that?" Robbie said.

"I guess I kind of thought of the two of us as best friends," Tig said.

"I thought we were all best friends," Olivia said. "All of us."

"We are," Tig said. "But . . . I don't know. I just . . . Robbie has always seemed to really get me, and we've always gotten along so well, and she's so cool . . . the coolest person in school."

"I'd have to agree with that," said Claire.

"And it made me feel cool that Robbie was my friend. And, well, I kind of thought . . . It sounds so stupid. . . ."

"Thought what?" Robbie said. "Spit it out."

"I thought I was your favorite," said Tig. It sounded even more stupid out loud than it had in her head, which was probably why Robbie started snickering. "Don't laugh," Tig said. "I feel ridiculous enough already."

"You've got to admit it's pretty kindergartenish," Robbie said. "I'm not supposed to be friends with anybody but you?"

"No, you can still be friends with us," said Olivia. "As long as Tig's your *favorite*." Everyone started giggling. Even Tig.

"Okay, okay, okay," Robbie said, and everyone got

quiet again. "So now we know your motive. But I still don't like that you had it in for Paris."

"I know," Tig said.

"You said I set your teeth on edge?" Paris said.

"Something like that," said Tig. "I don't remember my exact wording."

"I'm sorry, P," said Robbie.

"Well, it's kind of hard to be mad at her for hating me because I'm so beautiful and talented," Paris said. She laughed. "I mean, I'm just sayin'."

Everyone giggled again. Tig was shocked. Paris was being so cool about it all and was letting her off the hook. She didn't have to. Paris had every right to be angry and could have easily used this opportunity to turn Robbie against her.

"Now I really feel bad," said Tig. "Paris, I didn't give you a chance, and I was wrong. I hope you can forgive me, and I hope we can be friends." She looked around at the other girls. "All of us. No favorites."

The other girls smiled. "Works for me," Olivia said.

"Me too," Claire said. "Robbie and Paris?"

CHAPTER TWENTY-SIX

Paris shrugged. "Shoot, far as I'm concerned, it's yesterday's cornbread."

Everyone looked at Robbie for the translation. "She means she considers this whole misunderstanding ancient history." The girls nodded.

"What about you, Robbie?" Olivia said. "Can you look at it as old cornbread too?"

"I don't know," Robbie said. "Tig, I still can't believe you would think that my bringing Paris into the band was some sort of evil plot to take over the world. That ticks me off."

"I know," said Tig. "That wasn't fair. But it did all fall into place rather neatly. You can see where I might have wondered, can't you?"

"Maybe. But you should have just asked me instead of talking about me behind my back. And what's this 'showing us who's boss' business?"

"I don't think those were my exact words," Tig said. "But whatever words I used, just know that they were said in anger. I should have just come to you and been honest. Can you forgive me?"

Robbie paused a moment before saying, "I guess I don't have much choice. I mean, seeing as how you're the boss and all."

Tig threw a pillow at her. Robbie threw it back. Then Paris picked one up and threw it at Tig also, followed by Olivia and Claire doing the same. "I give! I give!" Tig said. "I'm *so* not the boss!"

"Can we eat now?" Olivia said. "Tension makes me hungry."

"Everything makes you hungry," said Robbie. "And yet you're still a stick."

"I know," said Olivia. "So let's eat!"

As they gorged on the pasta dish Mrs. Ripley had prepared for supper, Tig wished she could just erase everything that had happened that night with Kyra. She was so relieved that her friends had forgiven her, and she was especially blown away by Paris's generosity about the whole thing. She hated to bring any of it up again. But just because the girls had been willing to sweep her mistake under the rug didn't change the fact that something had to be done about Kyra.

"Guys, what about Kyra?" Tig asked. "What's our next move there?"

"Yeah, that's a tough one," Olivia said. "I mean, I know I was all, 'Let's try to see things from her point of view,' but sheesh! She was so vindictive tonight. It seemed kind of like she enjoyed the whole scene."

"I agree," said Claire. "I'd never seen that side to Kyra before. It kind of makes me afraid to be friends with her."

"Yeah," said Robbie, "I'm not a fan of temper tantrums. That was not cool."

"So what do you suggest we do?" Tig asked.

"Ignore her," Robbie replied. "Like a mom who walks off from a kicking and screaming toddler."

"Aww, I think y'all need to cut the girl some slack," said Paris. "If my parents were splitting up, I'd be pretty messed up too."

"I guess you're right," said Olivia. "But I've got my own problems without Kyra's drama."

"What problems?" asked Paris. "Is everything okay?"

"It's my boyfriend, Will," said Olivia.

Tig tried not to look too interested, but her stomach flipped when Will's name was mentioned. Tig thanked her lucky stars she hadn't told Kyra or anyone else about that day in the hall last year. Before Will had asked Olivia out, he'd all but told Tig he couldn't stop thinking about her. And thank goodness she hadn't confessed to Kyra that, ever since school had started this year, she couldn't stop thinking about Will, either.

"What's up with Will?" asked Robbie. "You guys break up?"

"No," said Olivia.

"What, then? Is he being a jerk?" Paris asked.

"Not at all," Olivia replied. "He's as sweet as can be."

"Then what's the problem?" asked Claire.

"That's just it," said Olivia. "I don't really know. I can't put my finger on it. I guess it's woman's intuition. I can just feel that something's not right. Things are sort of weird with him."

"Weird how?" asked Tig.

"I don't know if I can point to any specific thing," said Olivia. "I just have this strange feeling that he's not as into me as I am into him."

"And you don't know why you feel that way?" asked Robbie.

"No, and that's what's so strange. It's not that he's ever rude or even distant. But I'm just so crazy about him, you know? I mean, I think about him all the time! And when we're together, I can hardly stop looking at him, he's so gorgeous. And I want to hold his hand or touch his arm or tell him how much I like him constantly!"

"And he doesn't feel the same?" Claire said.

"I don't think so," said Olivia. "I think he likes me just fine, but he's not crazy about me. Like, I mean, I can't see him standing out in a rainstorm and telling me it's not over and then passionately kissing me and refusing to ever let me go."

"For crying out loud, this is middle school, not *The Notebook*," said Robbie.

"Maybe I expect too much, or want too much," said Olivia. "Maybe I just don't know how guys are supposed to act with their girlfriends because I've never had a boyfriend before Will. But I just don't think he's at the same level about me as I am about him. I wonder sometimes . . . do you think maybe he likes someone else?"

Tig almost choked on her pasta. "Went down the wrong pipe," she said when everyone looked at her.

"I'm sure it's nothing like that," Claire said.

"Yeah, some guys are just not capable of being swept away," said Paris. "My sister, Jade, is seventeen, and she's had a lot of boyfriends."

"Are her boyfriends like Will?" Olivia asked. "Nice but kind of . . . distant?"

"I wouldn't say distant," said Paris. "But some guys are less showy about how they feel. That's not always a bad thing, though. You really don't want a guy who can't live without you. Those guys are clingy and needy and it's just not good. Not good at all."

"Ooh!" said Robbie. "Like that guy who got down on his knees and begged Jade not to break up with him?"

Paris groaned. "How uncomfortable was that?!"

"You guys were there?" Claire said.

"Yes," said Robbie. "It was the most pathetic thing I've ever seen. Big linebacker, sobbing like a baby in their living room, begging Jade to take him back. Promising he'd do anything she said if she'd give him another chance."

"Eww," said Tig. "Did she take him back?"

"No way," said Paris. "I think all he did was remind her why she broke up with him in the first place."

"Why are some people so desperate to be loved?" asked Claire.

"We could ask Kyra that," said Tig. "I swear, at least once a week with her, it's 'I wish I had a boyfriend' or 'Why doesn't Crush of the Week like me back?' Not hearing all that constantly may be the one upside of her not speaking to us."

"And to think, Olivia," said Robbie, "you were going to find the perfect guy for each of us. Kyra really blew her chance, huh?" She laughed.

"Wait a minute," said Paris. "Maybe that's it."

"What's it?" asked Robbie.

"Look, I know y'all are mad at Kyra," said Paris.

"And to be a hundred percent honest, she hasn't exactly won me over with her carrying-on tonight. But she's going through a terrible time right now. And when it comes down to it, blood's always thicker than water, and she's Tig's cousin. No matter how mad Tig is right now, there's no changing that. This has to get resolved; they can't feud forever. Robbie, you said Kyra's acting like a toddler, and you know what all toddlers want? Attention. Tig, you said she's dying to have a boyfriend. So it seems to me like all we need to do to get her to straighten up and fly right is to find her a fella."

"Problem is," said Tig, "all the guys at school kind of know what Kyra's like. They can smell the desperation on her. It's not attractive."

"All the guys at *your* school know what Kyra's like," Paris said with a raised eyebrow and a grin. "But not the guys at my school."

Chapter Twenty-Seven

The girls spent the next hour logged in to Paris's social media accounts as they launched Operation Find Kyra a Boyfriend.

"What about this one?" Paris asked. The girls looked at his photos and read his profile.

"He's cute," said Tig. "But all these pictures are of hunting and fishing. Kyra's an animal lover. She'd hate that."

"I'd bet money that if she thought he was interested," said Robbie, "she'd be out in the deer stand with him."

Tig smiled. "You're probably right," she said. "But if this plan is going to work, we've got to find Kyra the perfect guy. Then she'll forget about being mad at us, feel better about her parents, and get happy again. Then we can put this drama behind us once and for all."

"What about this one?" Paris asked.

Tig looked at the photo. "He looks all right," she said. "What's his story?" Tig read his profile. "What is he, a genius or something? Looks like he's the president of every academic club in your whole school."

"Pretty much," said Paris.

"What makes you think he'd be a good match for Kyra?" asked Robbie.

"For starters, I think he'd be interested in her," Paris said.

"Why's that?" asked Tig.

"He's kind of girl crazy," said Paris. "I think he's asked out almost every girl in eighth grade, and even a few seventh graders."

"So he gets around a lot?" Robbie said.

"No, that's just it," said Paris. "He asks, but they say no."

"Has he asked you out?" said Olivia.

"Oh yeah," said Paris.

"And what did you say?" asked Claire.

"I told him no way," Paris said. "It was the homecoming dance last year, and I said no for a couple of different reasons. First of all, my daddy's not about to have me going on dates in middle school. So I couldn't have gone even if I'd wanted to."

"And why didn't you want to?" asked Claire.

"Because," said Paris, "he'd already asked four other girls ahead of me. I couldn't have said yes; it was a matter of self-respect. I don't play second fiddle."

"Or fifth fiddle, apparently," said Robbie.

"All right, let's say your dad would've allowed you to go to the dance with him and he'd asked you first. Would you have said yes then?" asked Tig.

"No," Paris replied.

"Why not? What's wrong with him?" Robbie said. "He's not uncute."

"Milo's . . . I don't know . . . different," said Paris. "I just don't need a guy who tries that hard. Besides, he's hard for me to talk to."

"What does he do, sit there and talk about nuclear physics?" said Robbie.

"Not exactly," said Paris, "but I'm sure he could if he wanted to. It's more like he just can't help but put some geniusy spin on everything. Like one day, somebody was talking about some murder story he'd seen on the news, and Milo started comparing it to some novel the seniors in high school have to read for the advanced placement class—something Russian, a hard-to-pronounce writer's name."

"Dostoyevsky? *Crime and Punishment?*" Robbie asked.

Tig laughed. "Maybe somebody else we know would be a better match for him," she said. Robbie lightly shoved her.

"Yeah, I think that was the name of it," said Paris. "And nobody knew what to say, because, of course, none of us knew what he was talking about. So everybody just kind of stopped talking after that and wandered off in different directions. I mean, the guy knows how to clear a room."

"So does Tig!" Robbie said. "Hey, maybe she's the better match! Tig, you could play 'Gotcha' for him!"

"*Burn!*" said Olivia.

"Shut up, Chan!" Tig said, even though she couldn't help but laugh a little.

"Oh, you guys, it's too soon," Claire said. "Don't make Tig feel bad about that again!"

"What are y'all talking about?" asked Paris.

"Just my public humiliation last spring when I tried to throw together a show when Claire was sick and Robbie was out of town. It didn't go well."

"I'm sorry," said Robbie. "I couldn't resist."

"You owed me one," said Tig. "Fair is fair."

"Anyway, back to this Milo fellow," said Claire.

"Yeah," said Paris. "So he's super-intellectual—there's that. But also, he's so honest."

"Honest is good, isn't it?" asked Olivia.

"Not always," said Paris. "See, Milo's really good

at math. I mean *really* good. He's gotten a perfect score on the math section of every standardized test we've ever taken. One time the governor even came to present him an award because of it. And I think because he's so good at math, he thinks everything is just a problem to solve. He doesn't know how to leave well enough alone, so he keeps on running his mouth even when he oughta hush up. Like that time he called me and asked me to homecoming. Do you know what he told me?"

"What?" the girls asked.

"He said, 'I've already asked four other girls who said no, and you were the next girl on my list.'"

The girls started giggling.

"No, he did not!" Olivia said, aghast.

"Oh yes, he did," said Paris.

"And yet you were able to resist him?" Robbie said. "A charmer like that?"

"See? That's what I mean," said Paris. "He doesn't know how to play it cool or flirt or hang back. His brain is so big, it's like everything is an equation, and he's got to solve it the quickest way there is."

"What makes you think he'd want to solve Kyra's equation?" asked Tig.

"Well," said Paris, "Kyra's cute. I think he'd go for her in a second."

"But would she go for him?" asked Claire.

"He's not bad-looking," said Robbie. "And Kyra's all about what other people think. Since she's not at Paris's school, she wouldn't know that Milo isn't considered cool. She'd give him a chance and get to know him. Sounds to me like they could both benefit from a clean slate."

"Good point," said Tig. "I just wonder if they'd have anything in common."

"That's the best part," Paris said. "That's what made me think of him. Kyra's bummed about failing at music, and Milo, smart as he is, actually failed at something recently."

"What? Curing cancer?" asked Robbie.

Paris laughed. "No, but something almost as serious down here in the South: football."

"Really?" asked Olivia.

"Yep. He went out for the team and didn't make the cut. Probably the only thing in his life he wasn't the best at. I'm sure it stung. So he and Kyra have that in common—they both got cut from something because they didn't measure up. I think they'd understand each other."

"I think it's worth a try," said Tig. "Now, how do we go about introducing them?"

"I know just what we'll do," said Paris.

Chapter Twenty-Eight

"I don't think it needs to be that soon," Tig said.

"Why not?" asked Paris. "The strings concert on Thursday night is a perfect opportunity. Milo will be the lead soloist."

"First of all, how would we get Kyra there?" Tig said. "She just dropped a pretty big bomb on us. It doesn't make sense for us to turn around the next day and say, 'Oh, by the way, how'd you like to join us for some lovely violin music?' "

"What did you have in mind?" asked Paris.

"May I?" asked Tig, gesturing to the laptop. Paris

handed it over. Tig began typing a message to Milo:

Hey, Milo. I'm in this new band with some girls from Lakeview Heights. Our drummer has a cousin I think you'd really like. Her name is Kyra Bennett. Feel free to PM her and tell her I'm a mutual friend. Have a good weekend! ☺

Tig hit send.

"Why didn't I think of that?" asked Paris.

"Well, you might have thought that, ordinarily, it would freak a girl out to get a PM from a guy she's never met," Tig said. "But in Kyra's case, given the fact that she basically has zero friends right now, I think this could work."

"Glad that's settled," Robbie said. "All this talk about chasing boys makes me feel very disempowered."

"Yes, let's talk about something else," said Claire.

"Agreed," said Olivia. "Enough about Milo. So, who do y'all think Will might like instead of me?

"Ugh!" said Robbie.

Yes, Tig thought. *Ugh, indeed.*

Chapter Twenty-Nine

"**G**ood morning," her mother said when Tig dragged herself into the kitchen the next day. It was not quite ten o'clock; the rest of the girls were still sleeping.

"Morning," said Tig. She poured herself a glass of milk, squirted in some chocolate syrup, and stirred.

"I saw that Kyra came by with Nick last night," said Mrs. Ripley.

"That she did," said Tig.

"I was hoping maybe that was a good sign. Not so much?"

"The only reason she showed up was so she could

try to get everyone mad at me," said Tig. "She told them I'd bad-mouthed Paris behind her back."

"Did you really do that?"

"Yep."

"Yikes," said Mrs. Ripley. "I hope that you learned something from this. You shouldn't say unkind things about other people."

"You mean like how you told Mrs. Leonard that Mrs. Beal never shuts up at the PTA meetings because she thinks she knows everything?"

Tig's mother blushed. "Touché," she said. "Do as I say, not as I do." She tousled Tig's hair. "How did Paris and the other girls take this revelation?"

"Surprisingly awesomely," said Tig. "Paris wasn't even mad. She's way cooler than I realized. I think I see now why Robbie likes her so much."

"That's good to hear," said Mrs. Ripley.

"Did Uncle Nick say anything to you about Kyra's being mad at me?"

"A little."

"Is he mad at me too?"

"Honey, no one likes for their children to be hurt. But you know your uncle Nick. He's easygoing. He sees it as a misunderstanding that will work itself out eventually. Besides, he's got enough to worry about with the divorce right now. Plus, I think he understands that Kyra never practiced and wasn't really good at playing bass. He's not holding a grudge against you."

"At least there's that," Tig said.

Tig's dad came into the kitchen. "You tell her about the new gig?" he said, kissing Mrs. Ripley on the cheek.

"What new gig?" Tig asked.

"I forgot all about it," said her mom.

"Your granddad's class reunion," said Mr. Ripley. "They want you to play at the country club. BD's so proud of you, he could pop."

"Are they going to pay us and everything?" Tig asked.

"Of course," said her dad. "How does three hundred dollars sound?"

Tig quickly did the math in her head. "That's sixty bucks apiece!"

"What about BD's agent's fee?" said her dad. "He's the one who got you the job, and he talked them up from the two hundred they originally wanted to pay y'all."

"What's an agent's fee?" Tig asked.

"Typically about fifteen percent, isn't it, Dave?" Tig's mom said.

"Yes, I think that's about the going rate," he replied.

Tig grabbed a piece of paper and a pencil out of the junk drawer. "Let's see . . . 300 times 0.15 would be 45 dollars for BD, which would leave 300 minus that 45, which is 255, divided by five, leaves 51 dollars apiece, which is, hey, still not that bad."

Tig's parents began to laugh.

"What? Did I do the math wrong?"

"You don't really think your granddad is going to charge you an agent's fee, do you?" her dad said. "I was just pulling your leg!"

"So we still get sixty bucks each?" Tig said. "I've got to tell the other girls!"

When she got to her room, Olivia, Claire, and Paris

were awake but lying on their sleeping bags. Robbie, however, was still out cold.

"Guess what, guess what, guess what," Tig said.

"Shh!" Claire said. "Robbie's still sleeping."

Tig leaped onto the air mattress, shaking Robbie. "Wake up! I have news!"

Robbie rolled over. "What?" she said. "This better be good."

"Oh, it's good," Tig said. "What if I told you that denim jacket you've had your eye on for two months is almost within your grasp?"

Robbie sat up. "I'm listening."

"We've been asked to play a gig. Three hundred dollars. That's sixty apiece. And no agent's fee."

"What's an agent's fee?" asked Claire.

"What's an agent?" said Paris.

"We have an agent?" said Olivia.

"What gig?" Robbie asked.

"My grandfather's high-school class reunion. At the country club."

"Ooh! The country club!" said Olivia. "Does our

fee include food? Their food is soooo good!"

"You and your stomach," said Robbie. "So, when do the old people get down? What's the date?"

"I don't know," said Tig. "I forgot to ask. Be right back." Tig ran downstairs, got the date from her parents, and ran back up. "The twenty-fourth of next month," she said. "It starts at six."

"And since they're pushing, what? Eighty? We should be done by seven thirty, tops," said Robbie.

"Hey, BD and my grandma, Mimi, are pretty spry," said Tig. "They stay up till nine thirty sometimes."

"We should be able to get a short set down in plenty of time," said Robbie. "If we all promise to practice daily."

The girls all agreed, then texted their parents. No one had any conflicts.

"Then it's on!" said Tig. "I'll call BD right now and tell him to book us!"

Chapter Thirty

Tig called BD from the den while the girls got dressed. He answered the phone in his Donald Duck voice. "Hew-wo?"

Tig giggled. "Hey, BD. What's up?"

"The sky," he replied. "The ceiling? The Goodyear blimp?" Ah, grandfather jokes. Tig laughed anyway to be polite.

"I meant, what are you and Mimi up to this morning?"

"Nothing really. Did your parents tell you about the reunion?"

"Yes!" said Tig. "How exciting!"

"Then you'll do it?"

"Yes, sir. All the girls are over at my house right now. We had a sleepover. They've all asked their parents, and everyone can make it, so we're good to go."

"That's great news," said BD. "I'll tell the committee they can print the invitations, then. Oh, won't this be fun?"

"We can hardly wait," said Tig. "How long will we need to play?"

"Only about an hour," said BD. "It's not much money, so they don't expect much. Plus, they understand that you're kids, and they don't want to work you too hard."

"That's nice of them," said Tig.

"Also, they realize that we can't take too much loud music or dancing at our age, anyway. But you girls realize you'll have to play some music from our class's generation, right? We're too old for all that clanging mess you kids today listen to."

"We've got plenty of time to learn some new

songs," said Tig. "Maybe you could select some of your favorites? And since you played in a band yourself back in the day, maybe you could choose some that don't have really difficult percussion parts. Would you mind?"

"It would be my pleasure," said BD. "I'll see if your Mimi has any requests too. But I won't let her pick anything too hard."

"Great," Tig replied. "Just text or email me the songs you have in mind and I'll run them by the other girls."

"Will do," he said. Then, once again in the Donald Duck voice, he said, "Good-bwye!"

"Bye, BD," said Tig.

While the girls had breakfast, Tig received an email from BD with his song choices. She and the other girls read the list. "I've never even heard of most of these," said Tig.

"Me neither," said Robbie. "And the ones I have heard of, I don't want to play. Sonny and Cher? Seriously? Not happening."

" 'The Twist'?" said Claire. "Doesn't that have a saxophone in it? We don't have a sax."

"What's this one?" asked Olivia. They looked it up on the Internet.

The girls looked at one another in complete horror as they took in a black-and-white image of a man in a cowboy hat and listened to him narrate a story about a coal miner who gave his life in an accident to save his fellow workers. Robbie almost fell over laughing. "Your granddad thinks a bunch of eighth-grade girls are going to be able to do this with a straight face?"

"That accent!" said Olivia. "This is country music!"

"Definitely not a rock song," said Tig.

"I'm not doing that," said Claire. "That's not even singing. It's talking. I'd feel ridiculous."

"Your granddad has some weird taste in music," said Robbie.

"I thought the sixties were supposed to be full of great music," said Tig. "What is this stuff he picked?"

"Apparently the British Invasion happened after your grandparents' class graduated," said Robbie. "But

still . . . we've got to be able to find some better songs
than these!"

The girls spent some time looking up music critics'
lists of the best songs of the early 1960s. Not finding
much they liked, they widened their search to include
the entire decade. Olivia liked one song that featured
an electric piano. It also had a cool bass line, but Paris
was worried she might not be able to master it in time
because of the offbeat rhythm.

The next song they looked at was "For Your Love,"
which seemed to have doable percussion, except for a
crazy break that would require some serious practice.
Then they selected the Beatles' "Twist and Shout" and
"I'm a Believer" by the Monkees, a group whose TV
show Olivia and Tig remembered seeing old reruns of
a few times.

"Is Paris going to be able to handle these? That's
three new songs by next month," said Tig. She looked
at Paris. "Not that I lack confidence in your abilities; I
just don't want to overwhelm you."

"Besides a little bit of guitar training, P's got two

things Kyra didn't," Robbie said. "A natural rhythm and the desire to go for it. I can show her the frets and come up with some simple arrangements. We'll have to pare it down, of course—no walking, no fills, nothing fancy—just quarter notes on the beat. What do you think, Paris?"

"Sure," she said.

The last song, which Robbie suggested for its straightforward bass line, was Stevie Wonder's "Signed, Sealed, Delivered." It was from 1970, but they figured their audience at the class reunion would still like it.

"If we can make these four happen," Tig said, "add them to the Stones song we've already got, plus 'Sweet Home Alabama,' that's six oldies songs we could play."

"We could also do that Sex Pistols song," said Robbie. "It's seventies punk, but we know it."

"Paris doesn't," Tig said. "That's one more song to put on her."

"I don't mind," said Paris. "I'm really enjoying learning the bass."

"If you think so, it's fine by me. Even though I doubt they're punk fans, I guess that song's slow enough that it wouldn't kill any of the old people," said Tig. "Good thing we won't have to play for more than an hour, so I guess seven songs isn't too bad. I say we do it."

"Let's get in one good practice before everyone has to leave," said Robbie.

The girls went out to the studio and got to work.

Tig was amazed at how quickly Paris picked things up. The guitar lessons she'd taken in elementary school had not been wasted.

It was amazing how much more the band could accomplish when all the members were dedicated. Tig could hardly stand the excitement. Sure, it was a bunch of grandparents, but it was a real show with a real—albeit short—set list. And real money! They were actually going to get paid for playing music!

Tig was so happy, she almost stopped worrying about the problem with Kyra.

Almost.

Chapter Thirty-One

On Sunday, Tig got a call from Paris.

"It's working," she said.

"What? The new songs? You're getting them down already?"

"No. I mean, yes, I'm working on that, too . . . but the other thing. The plan. The Kyra and Milo thing."

"Oh!" said Tig. "What's going on?"

"Milo sent me a message that he'd introduced himself to Kyra on chat," Paris said. "Apparently, they've been talking some. He likes her, I think."

"Does she like him?"

"Well, it's hard to say. I mean, Milo's a guy. Guys think they're doing great with girls even when they're not. Especially Milo . . . I told you he's not good at picking up hints."

"But if she's talking to him, that's a good sign," Tig said. "I wish we knew what she'd said, though. She might have politely blown him off."

"I don't think so," said Paris. "Milo said she's coming to the strings concert on Thursday to hear him play."

"Get out of here!" said Tig. "Wow, that was fast!" The more she thought about it, though, it wasn't that surprising. Kyra was probably giddy over a mystery boy's interest in her. In fact, Kyra was probably bursting right this very minute to call Tig and tell her all about it. Well, good. Let her burst. "Thanks for the heads-up," Tig said. "It will be interesting to see how Kyra acts at school tomorrow."

That Monday morning, Kyra came into the gym after Tig, Robbie, Olivia, and Claire were already seated. But instead of walking right past them to go sit with the Scholars' Bowl team, she walked up to the Pandora's Box girls, her posture and facial expression sheepish, to say the least. "Hi," she said.

"Don't I know you from somewhere?" Tig said. "Oh right. You look just like this cousin of mine who tried to ruin my life over the weekend."

Kyra grimaced. "Sorry?" she said.

"Yes, it was pretty sorry of you," said Tig. "But Paris is still speaking to me . . . no thanks to you."

"I really am sorry," said Kyra. "That was a rotten thing to do to you. And to Paris. But I was so upset about the band. You hurt my feelings, and I wanted to hurt you back."

"Mission accomplished," said Tig.

"Can we just forget it ever happened?" Kyra said. "I don't know what got into me. Lately stuff just really sets me off. I know I overreacted."

Tig couldn't help but feel a little sorry for Kyra. If she were going through what Kyra was, she'd probably have some major mood swings too. She'd probably just be looking for an excuse to lash out at anyone who was nearby. And even though Tig was still angry, she thought of how quickly Paris had forgiven *her*. It seemed somehow like she ought to at least try to extend the same generosity. "I guess we can try to move past it," Tig said. "If you can understand that we didn't ask you to leave the band out of meanness. You know we didn't. And if you understand that I didn't tell the girls about your parents until they'd already heard about it somewhere else."

"I know," said Kyra. "I understand. And I'm over it. Really, I am. Can we all be friends again?"

"What about the Scholars' Bowl team?" asked Robbie. Tig was glad she wasn't letting her off the hook too easily.

"Oh, y'all," Kyra said. "I can't hang with them. They have conversations about world geography and European history. I've never felt so dumb."

"So you've come back to your intellectual equals?" said Tig.

"Yeah," said Kyra. "Except for Robbie and Claire,

of course." Kyra smiled.

"Oh, thanks!" Olivia said. "Thanks so much!"

But at least they were laughing together again, even if it was awkward, tentative laughter.

"Hey, we're really sorry about your folks," Robbie said.

"Yeah," said Olivia. "That stinks."

"We want to be here for you," said Claire. "If you'll let us."

Kyra hugged them all. "Thanks. It helps. Really. I'm so sorry we fought. I need y'all! Losing my family is hard enough. I can't lose my friends, too." Her voice cracked a bit and she swallowed hard. "And, Robbie, I'm sorry I was so ugly to Paris. She deserves better. She's so nice. Really, really nice. And thoughtful!"

Robbie grinned. "Is she? What makes you say so?"

"Well," said Kyra, a twinkle in her eye, "she introduced me online to someone from her school."

"You don't say?" said Tig.

"Yes," said Kyra. "His name is Milo and he's amazing! He's cute and he's supersmart."

"I thought you were tired of smart people?" Robbie said.

"Not the hot ones who are into me," Kyra replied. "Y'all, he's the top student in his class and he plays the violin and he's so charming!"

"How so?" asked Tig.

"Well, in one of our first messages, he told me I was pulchritudinous. Isn't that sweet?"

"Pulchri-what-i-what?" asked Tig.

"Beautiful," Robbie explained. But Tig didn't think the word sounded beautiful at all. More like a skin infection or something.

"I'm going to his strings concert on Thursday, and then I'll get to meet him in person!" Kyra said. "And it's all because of Paris!"

"Paris's pretty killer," said Robbie.

"I'm happy for you," said Tig.

"We all are," said Claire.

"And you guys were right to kick me out of the band," said Kyra. "I'm a lousy bass player. And I never practiced. You'll be better off without me."

"Let's just move forward from here," Tig said. She knew it would take some time for things to be the same again, if they ever would. Kyra had violated her trust and had shown a pretty severe mean streak. Those weren't things Tig would easily forget. But Kyra was dealing with a lot right now, and besides, she was family. And an awkward friendship with her cousin was better than no friendship with her at all.

"You can still come to practice just to hang out with us if you want," Claire said. "Right, Tig?"

"Sure," Tig said.

"Oh, thanks," said Kyra. "But I can't make it. I've got Milo's concert."

Kyra took her former usual seat and told the girls every detail she could think of about Milo. Meanwhile, Will came in and sat with Olivia. "Silly!" Olivia said. "Your shirt!"

The girls looked at Will's shirt. He'd buttoned it wrong and it hung crooked.

Will blushed. "I was kind of running late this morning," he said.

"I think it's adorable!" Olivia said. "Isn't he adorable?"

Robbie made a gag face, and the other girls laughed. Tig laughed too, but the problem was, she agreed with Olivia.

It was a weird feeling. Part of Tig wanted Will to be perfectly happy with Olivia because Olivia was her friend, and Olivia was crazy about Will. But the other part of Tig hoped that Will couldn't stop thinking about her any more than she could stop thinking about him.

It seemed to Tig that now that they were in eighth grade, so much of life seemed to center around boys. She thought back to when they were in elementary school and thought boys had cooties. Things were so uncomplicated back then. But when she stole a quick glance at Will and he smiled at her and her stomach flipped, it wasn't necessarily a feeling she entirely disliked. Even though it was something of a slow torture—thinking about Will all the time but not being able to do anything about it, wondering if he felt the same way—Tig wasn't sure she wanted this strange torture to end. It was like having a beautifully wrapped box you hadn't opened yet. The possibility, the expectation, the curiosity, the longing . . . Could what was actually inside the box ever measure up? Something about this odd, new emotion drew her. It made her feel alive.

Chapter Thirty-Two

Thursday afternoon practice went incredibly well once again with Kyra out and Paris in. The progress the girls made was steady and came much faster than ever before. They were all feeling pretty good about the class reunion they'd be playing at the end of next month. There was very little anxiety that they'd be able to pull it off; rather, they all felt confident that the gig would be a huge success.

Tig reveled in the way the band was thriving. It was the first time since she'd started Pandora's Box that everything finally seemed to be coming together. She was able to relax and really enjoy playing the drums and having a band. Now that Tig no longer had to ride Kyra about practicing or make excuses for her to Robbie and the other girls, it was as though a huge weight had been taken off her shoulders. Finally Tig could enjoy the whole rock band experience.

While the girls were taking a quick break, Tig remembered something she'd wanted to show them. "Take a look at this," she said, passing her phone to Olivia. It was a text from BD with a photo of the reunion invitation.

The invitation was cute and colorful, and Tig was excited to point out the line that said, *Special performance by Pandora's Box*.

"See how they put our band name on there?" Tig said. "Pretty cool, huh? I don't know. . . . Something about seeing it in print makes it seem more real." Olivia admired the photo, then passed Tig's phone around so the other girls could look. Claire and Paris oohed and ahhed just like Olivia had. Only Robbie noticed.

"Um, you guys," Robbie said. "Did you notice the

asterisk next to the words 'Pandora's Box'?"

"Oh yeah," Tig said. "They put all of our names in small print at the bottom of the invite."

"Not exactly *all* of *our* names," said Robbie. She passed the phone back to Tig, the invitation photo enlarged, and scrolled over the bottom.

"Oh no," said Tig.

"Oh no what?" asked Olivia. "What's the matter?"

Tig groaned. "I'm so sorry, y'all. I totally forgot to tell BD."

"Tell him what?" asked Claire. Tig passed her the phone. "Oh," Claire said. "Yikes."

"What is it?" asked Paris. Claire passed her the phone. "Oh, is that all?" Paris said. "Not a big deal."

"Yes, it is," said Robbie. "They put Kyra's name instead of yours."

"It's not like any of those old folks will know the difference," Paris said. "Don't make a muffin out of a molehole."

"It's 'a mountain out of a molehill,' " said Olivia.

"I know. I just like mine better," said Paris. "There's

no broadband out in the country. We make things up to amuse ourselves."

"Can you call your grandfather and have him make the correction?" Robbie said. "Paris's laid-back, but I still want her to get proper credit. She's working really hard as our bass player."

"Agreed," said Tig. "I'll call BD right now. They've already mailed the invitations, but maybe they can send out a correction or at least have it corrected at the reunion." Tig walked outside the studio and called her grandfather. She explained how the girls had replaced Kyra with Paris. "So, if you could send out a correction or whatever . . ."

"I'm afraid it's not going to be that easy," said BD.

"Why not?" said Tig. "Is it the postage cost? You don't really have to mail anything else. . . . Just change the names on the signs or whatever at the reunion."

"It's not postage," BD said. "It's Kyra. I don't know if this show will work without her."

"Why wouldn't it?" Tig asked. Sure, BD had always been nice to Kyra, but she was on Tig's mom's side of the family, and BD was Tig's father's dad. It wasn't like Kyra was BD's granddaughter or anything. So why would he push for Kyra to perform at his reunion?

"It's complicated," BD said. "Mimi and I are out running errands. We'll swing by your house on the way home in a bit, and I'll explain it to you in person."

When Tig went back inside the studio, Robbie asked, "Did you get everything straightened out?"

"Not exactly," Tig replied. "I don't know what the big deal is, but BD's coming by in a while to explain it to me in person."

"What's to explain?" Robbie asked.

"I have no idea."

Olivia's mom pulled into the driveway. "Gotta run," Olivia said. "Let us know what's up when you know."

"I'm sure it's nothing that can't be worked out," Tig said.

After all the girls were gone and Tig was inside doing her homework, BD and Mimi arrived. Tig was relieved. The suspense was killing her, and she couldn't focus on her work; she'd read the same passage on her English worksheet three times already.

Once BD and Mimi had gotten all the hugs and hellos out of the way with Tig's younger sister and brother, Tig and her grandparents sat down on the sofa together while her mom continued cooking supper.

"So, what's the deal with the reunion performance?" Tig asked. "Why is Kyra even an issue?"

BD cleared his throat. "You remember my former high-school classmate Norman Allen, don't you?"

Tig had to think for a moment. "That weird-looking guy with the teeth?" She made her hand into a claw and held it in front of her mouth.

BD smiled. "That's the one."

"His teeth weren't that bad," said Mimi.

"You may have forgotten that he's Kyra's great-uncle's first cousin," said BD.

Of course Tig had forgotten that. Why should such a random fact take up valuable real estate in her brain? It wasn't like the man and Kyra were even close; Kyra barely knew him. Tig vaguely recalled seeing him around town here and there over the years as she was growing up and remembered her family exchanging pleasantries with him, but that was about it.

"Okay," Tig said. "But what's that got to do with anything?"

"Norman and I have never exactly been close friends," BD said. "He's had a grudge against me ever since I stole your Mimi away from him when we were young."

"You dated the teeth guy?" Tig said, scrunching up her face in horror. The question of whether they'd ever kissed briefly sped through Tig's mind, but she pushed it out immediately. The thought of her own grandmother kissing anyone, especially the teeth guy, was enough to activate her gag reflex.

"Not really," said Mimi. "It was never serious."

"He asked you to marry him!" BD said.

"Just that one time, sugar," Mimi replied. BD made a face. "I said no, didn't I?"

"Gross! You almost married the teeth guy?" Tig's mind then went to her own DNA and how she had come so close to inheriting those same teeth. She'd really dodged a bullet there.

"I certainly did not," said Mimi. "I told him he ought to go out with Angela Payton, and he did, and they got married and had a real nice family and I believe now they have seven grandchildren. Angela is real nice. Always was. You know, I knew her mama and daddy, and they were always real nice too. All of them. Her daddy worked at the pharmacy downtown, and—"

"Well, he may have married Angela, but he always carried a torch for Mimi," said BD.

"Oh, he did not," Mimi said, waving her hand.

"Did too!"

"This is all very interesting," Tig said. And it kind of was. It was like an old people soap opera. "But what does any of this have to do with the gig?"

"I was getting to that," said BD. "Norman was on the planning committee, and when I brought up your band playing, he said absolutely not. A middle-school band was too inexperienced, he said, and we ought to have some real musicians. Of course, he was only saying that because it was *my* idea and *my* granddaughter. But when I reminded him that *his* great-niece-cousin or whatever she is was in the band with you, well, then, of course, he got all puffed up about wanting to show her off, so he agreed to it."

"Oh," said Tig. "Now I get it." At least, she thought she did.

"As you can see," said BD, "if Kyra doesn't play with the band, we may have a problem."

"What if we don't say a word about it and just show up and play?" Tig said. "It will be too late for him to do anything about it then."

"Well, it would be," said BD, "except that this morning I got a call from Norman. He'd called your aunt Laurie to tell her how excited he was about Kyra playing his reunion, and your aunt Laurie informed him that Kyra had been kicked out of the band."

"That makes sense," Tig said. She knew Aunt Laurie would find some way to punish her for kicking Kyra out, even if Kyra was over it.

"So now Norman says if Kyra isn't playing with the band anymore, the deal is off," said BD.

"Does he have that kind of power?" Tig asked.

"I'm afraid so," said BD. "Two of the other men on the committee played on the football team with Norman, and one of the women is his wife's best friend. He has connections. I have some influence with the other committee members, but it could be close if we had to vote again."

"I see," said Tig. Who knew senior citizens had such power struggles?

"I'm sorry, Tigger," said BD. "I just don't know what to do."

Tig had a thought. "Maybe Mimi could call him and sweet-talk him?"

"I will do no such thing!" Mimi said. "I do not sweet-talk other women's husbands!"

"I'm just saying, I'm your granddaughter too," Tig said. Then she grinned and added, "Really, Mimi, this is all your fault for not marrying him fifty years ago." Tig and BD started giggling.

"Oh, hush up, you two," Mimi said, but she was giggling too.

"I was thinking that if you could let Kyra stay on as bass player just until this one performance is over, maybe Norman wouldn't raise a stink," said BD.

"I don't know," Tig said. After all the trouble she'd had with kicking Kyra out of the band, inviting her back in, even for just a short time . . . well, that might really be opening a Pandora's box. It seemed a shame to stir things back up now that the dust had just settled. Besides, even though she'd technically forgiven Kyra, Tig wasn't fully over the betrayal. Something like that would take a while to move past, if she ever could. The truth was, even though things were cool again with Tig and Kyra, Tig was glad to have her out of the band. If she let Kyra back in, even temporarily, there was a chance that Kyra might try to wheedle her way in again permanently. What if Tig had to kick her out twice? "I'll talk to the other girls in the band. I'll see what we can come up with."

When Mimi and BD left, Tig thought about earlier that afternoon when she'd felt all that weight taken off her shoulders.

Well, it had been nice while it had lasted.

Chapter Thirty-Three

Tig would have preferred to talk with Robbie, Paris, Olivia, and Claire face-to-face about all this, but there was no way she could sit on it overnight. She was bursting to get it off her chest. She hoped Robbie or one of the other girls would have some idea about what to do.

Tig set up a group video chat with her bandmates. Claire's hair was in a towel; Olivia's was held back from her face with a cloth band, and she had zit cream dotting spots along her forehead and nose. Robbie was wearing a ponytail, something she almost never did. Paris, however, was the most interesting of all: she was holding a baby goat.

"Is this the cutest critter you've ever seen or what?" Paris asked.

The girls squealed over the baby goat's cuteness for a few minutes, and then Tig got down to business. "No offense to your critter, P, but we've got a problem," she said.

"What's wrong?" asked Claire.

"It's the gig," Tig replied.

"They changed the date?" asked Robbie. "The pay? Are they going to try to pay us in tapioca pudding?"

"This isn't a joke," Tig said. "My grandparents told me tonight that one of the old men on the reunion committee is Kyra's great-uncle's first cousin. The only reason he voted to have us play is because of Kyra. Now he's found out she's no longer in the band and he wants to cancel us."

"Wow, get a life," Robbie said. "Old people have way too much time on their hands, obvs."

"My sentiments exactly," said Tig.

"I don't see what the big deal is," said Olivia. "They don't sound like very close relatives, so why does he care so much?"

"Apparently, this whole saga goes back several decades to when he was spurned by my grandma," said Tig. "He just wants to cause trouble for my granddad."

"That's strangely romantic," said Olivia. "He still hasn't gotten over your grandma? What is she, like, Cleopatra or somebody?"

"Who knew Mimi was such a hot ticket back in the day?" said Tig.

"I just had this weird thought," said Claire. "Someday we'll be old like they are, and then people who are the age we are now will have a hard time imagining us as young. Isn't that kind of sad to think about?"

"Yeah," said Olivia. "Someday the guys we think are so cute will be old men, and we'll be old ladies, and it will be like, what was the big deal about them?"

Tig took that in for a moment. She had a flash of herself and her friends as old women. What if Will and Olivia got married and had children and grand-children, and they all still lived in the same town, and every time Tig saw Will, she felt that same pang of regret mixed with jealousy that he belonged to Olivia? Could feelings really last that many years? Appar-ently, they could, given the Mimi/BD/Norman Allen triangle. But Tig could barely imagine herself in high school, let alone as a grandmother. She shook off the thought—it was something to ponder later, when the aspects of her current life were less pressing.

"So there's nothing we can do, then?" Robbie said. "It's over? There's no gig?"

"There is one thing we can do," said Tig. "But you're not going to like it. I don't."

"What?" asked Paris.

"Yeah, what?" said Robbie. "I've already mentally bought that denim jacket with the sixty bucks added to my stash. This gig needs to happen."

"BD says that if we leave Kyra in the band just until after this one gig, the old man won't pull the rug out from under us."

"You're right," said Robbie. "I don't like it."

"Me neither," said Claire. "Kicking Kyra out once was hard enough. I'd hate to have to do it twice."

"Exactly," said Tig. It was nice that Claire understood her feelings without her having to state them.

"Besides," said Olivia, "I hate to point out the obvious, but does anyone actually think that Kyra could learn all those new songs before the performance? I mean, she could barely play the ones we've been working on for months."

That hadn't occurred to Tig at all. "You're right," Tig said. "Olivia, I hadn't even thought about that. I was so focused on how weird it would be to invite her back in that I'd completely forgotten the most obvious problem. Kyra would never be able to get these songs together in time for the gig, and then we'd have no set list—not even an hour's worth."

"And we were scraping for that as it was," said Robbie.

"Yeah," said Claire.

"Paris, you haven't said much," said Tig. "How's all

this sitting with you?"

"Y'all know me," said Paris. "I'm easygoing. If you need to get Kyra back for this gig, I ain't gonna be mad at you. But I'm with Olivia. I doubt she could do it."

"Here's a thought," said Robbie. "What if we had Kyra play one or two of our old songs with us at the reunion, and then we sub in Paris after that? Then Kyra doesn't have to learn any new material, and the old guy still gets his third-cousin-twice-removed-great-grand-niece glory?"

"That's a great idea," said Claire.

"I agree," said Olivia.

"I knew you'd think of something," said Tig. "Paris, how does that sound to you?"

"Works for me," Paris said.

"Okay," Tig said. "Now all we have to do is get Kyra to agree to this."

"Good thing we already made up with her," said Robbie. "Can you imagine how awkward that would have been?"

Tig felt a wave of nausea just thinking about it. If

she hadn't already made up with Kyra and had to go begging to her about this gig, Kyra probably would've milked it for all it was worth. She knew how pouty and manipulative Kyra could be as well as she knew her own name. But the funny thing was, knowing this about Kyra had never stopped Tig from being close with her their entire lives—after all, Kyra had her good points, too, didn't she? With the betrayal still fresh in Tig's mind, it was getting harder to remember what those good points were. Tig decided that maybe everyone had a dark side if you got to know them well enough. But somehow that didn't make her feel any better about Kyra. Tig tried to remind herself about the divorce and how hard that was for Kyra, but was that supposed to be a get-out-of-jail-free card for every rotten thing Kyra did from here on out?

"Awkward. You can say that again," Tig said. "All right, if we're all agreed, I'll talk to Kyra about it tomorrow at school."

"Why don't you just call her tonight and get it over with?" asked Claire.

CHAPTER THIRTY-THREE

"It's getting late," said Tig. "I've still got some homework to finish."

But the truth was, Tig was in no hurry to talk to Kyra . . . or to spend any more time with her than she had to.

Chapter Thirty-Four

"**W**e need to talk," Tig said to Kyra the next morning in the gym.

"You're so right," said Kyra. "I've got to tell you everything Milo said in chat last night!"

Like I care, Tig wanted to say. It annoyed her that Kyra thought that everything with the two of them would go on without missing a beat. Like Tig would gloss right over her betrayal and they'd be just as close as they were before it. *Well, no,* Tig thought. *It's not that easy.*

Kyra prattled on about Milo for a good five

minutes, never seeming to notice that Tig wasn't really paying attention. When Kyra came up for air, Tig jumped in. "Your mom got your uncle or whatever he is—Norman—all stirred up about the reunion gig."

"Did she?" There was no *I'm sorry to hear that* in Kyra's tone. More of a *good for Mom* tone. Certainly there was no hint of surprise. Kyra's mother had always been one to stir things up whenever possible.

"Yes, she did," Tig said flatly. "Apparently, if you don't play, we lose the gig."

"Oh, how about that?"

Tig was furious. Not only was Kyra enjoying this, it appeared that she already knew all about it. Perhaps, Tig realized, she'd even put her mom up to it.

"Yes, how about that?" Tig said.

"So I guess you want me back in the band, then?"

"Temporarily," said Tig.

"Hmmm," said Kyra. "I'll have to think about it."

"Is that so?" said Tig. "Well, think about this, too, while you're at it: the Scholars' Bowl team could probably use a new member."

"What's that supposed to mean?"

"It means, Kyra, that you're lucky you have any friends at all after that stunt you pulled at the studio. We forgave you for that."

"And I forgave y'all for kicking me out of the band in the first place. By my accounting, we're even."

"Your accounting is way off, then," said Tig. "We kicked you out of the band because you left us no choice. You refused to practice. We tried to be nice about it. You, on the other hand, betrayed my trust and tried to turn my friends against me for no reason other than spite. It was hateful and mean and premeditated. But we gave you another chance. And this is how you thank us?"

"Well, when you put it that way, it sounds like it was all my fault!"

"It *was* all your fault!" Tig said. She could feel herself shaking with rage. "You know, Kyra, I'm sorry about Uncle Nick and your mom. I really am. But you don't get a free pass to act any way you want to just because of the divorce! I've tried to be understanding and patient because we're family, but family is about more than blood. Family is the way you treat one another. And if this is the best you can do, well . . . nothing says we have to be tight just because we're cousins. So just forget about the gig. And while you're at it, just forget about me, too."

"Tig!" Kyra called as Tig stormed out of the gym.

"Tig Ripley!" called the coach who supervised the gym. "The bell hasn't rung yet!"

She'd probably get detention for it, but Tig kept walking.

Chapter Thirty-Five

Tig seethed the rest of the morning. By algebra class, she was still ready to blow.

"Did you get written up for leaving the gym this morning?" Regan asked.

"No," said Tig. "Coach found me and gave me a warning, though."

"You're lucky," said Regan. "Hey, what's with you getting all rebel all of a sudden?"

"It was either leave the gym without permission or commit homicide," Tig said.

"Fight with your cousin?"

"You could say that, yes."

"Can't say I blame you," Regan said. "I've never liked her."

"Trust me, I know," said Tig. "She's been trying to get you to like her since elementary school." Tig let out a short laugh, then got serious. "Why is it that you've never liked her? I mean, she has tried so hard. She's done everything short of worship you."

"That's just it," Regan said. "She's a suck-up. She doesn't like *me*. She just likes my status. She thinks that if she's friends with me, she'll be popular."

"Isn't that how it works?" asked Tig.

Regan smiled. "Yeah, I guess so. Popularity by association. But who wants friends like that?"

"You have worse friends than Kyra," Tig said. "Haley's about as annoying as they come."

"No argument there," said Regan. "Haley can be a brat sometimes, but Haley's got something Kyra doesn't. Loyalty. The way Kyra came to me and offered to turn on you so she could get in with our group? Haley would never do something like that. Neither would Sofia."

Tig thought about this for a moment and decided Regan probably had a point. "She's my cousin, you know? That makes it so much worse."

"I'm sure," said Regan. "So what'd she do this time?"

As Tig told Regan the whole story about the gig and the way Kyra had acted that morning, it occurred to Tig that she was confiding in Regan Hoffman, of all people. Regan Hoffman, her biggest enemy from seventh grade. What was she thinking? Regan could not—*should not*—be trusted. Ever. But talking to her now didn't feel that way to Tig at all.

Will came in just before the bell rang. "Somebody I know's got some business to handle," he said. He grinned, making Tig's heart ache.

"What do you know about it?" Tig asked. It wasn't a smart comment but an actual question.

"Kyra's already told Olivia about it and Olivia's already told me," Will said. "According to Kyra, you bit her head off for no reason."

CHAPTER THIRTY-FIVE

Typical, Tig thought.

Will continued. "Now Olivia's worried the show is off, and she's dying to play it. You'd think sixty bucks was a million dollars. It would be a shame to cancel, though. I like your set list—I looked up all the songs. The drum solo at the bridge of 'For Your Love' is pretty sweet. You're going to nail it!" Then Will started singing the chorus, where the guy lists all the poetic and beautiful things he would give in exchange for the girl's love. As he sang, his eyes locked onto Tig's. She felt that electric shock that was by now so familiar, and forced herself to look away.

"It's not my fault if the show is off," Tig said abruptly.

Will stopped singing and shook his head. "Girls!"

"You know what you ought to do?" said Regan. "Just get her to play the one gig and then worry about whether you want to maintain the friendship. It sounds like this performance is pretty important to you and the other girls. Don't let Kyra ruin it for you."

"You're forgetting one major roadblock," said Tig.

"Kyra's holding the cards. She's not going to agree to play even one song unless I kiss her rear end."

"Sure she will," said Regan.

"What makes you say so?"

"Because I'll tell her to," said Regan. "She'll do anything I say."

Tig's mouth fell open. "You'd do that?"

"Of course," Regan said. "What are friends for?"

Friends? Regan Hoffman and Tig Ripley were now friends?

Chapter Thirty-Six

Magic.

That was what it was. Magic.

By English class two periods later, the whole drama about whether Kyra would play the reunion was, as Paris would've said, yesterday's cornbread.

And Tig hadn't even had to sweet-talk her.

One word from Regan, and Kyra had not only agreed to play the gig, she'd also apologized to Tig for the way she'd acted that morning. And she'd said she didn't want to play more than one song at the show *and* that she knew that would be the end of her association with Pandora's Box *and* she was fine with it. She further promised that there would be no more outbursts, manipulations, or wheedling of any kind to try to get back in. In fact, after Kyra's admission that the whole thing had been all her fault from the get-go—from not practicing and forcing Tig to kick her out of the band to the way she'd acted earlier that day in the gym— Kyra seemed to have no more interest whatsoever in discussing the band or anything to do with the band. And all this had happened before Mrs. Thompson even went over the bell-ringer activity. It was as though none of it had even happened.

Their English class was reading *Julius Caesar*, a Shakespeare play about ancient Romans who kill this guy Caesar because they think he's going to try to become king. One of the guys who stabs Caesar is his best friend, Brutus, so Mrs. Thompson made a whole big deal about the fact that Caesar feels totally betrayed by his friend. Tig sort of thought the whole getting-stabbed-to-death thing might be a bigger deal than betrayal, but she figured English teachers had to find something in stories besides the obvious if they wanted to keep their jobs.

For class that day, everyone had to get up and recite something they'd memorized from the play. They had a choice between a speech from Brutus, a speech from this other friend of Caesar who hadn't stabbed him, or a speech from Caesar about not fearing death. Tig had chosen the last one because it was the shortest.

" 'Cowards die many times before their deaths,' " Tig said when it was her turn. She didn't really mind having to speak in front of the class; no one was paying much attention anyway. And she sort of liked the message of her recitation: the guy was basically saying that there's no reason to fear death because it will happen at some point anyway, and if you sit around being scared of it, it's sort of like you're dying a little death all the time. Might as well quit thinking about it, live your life without worrying, and die just that once instead of a bunch of mini-deaths in your imagination.

"Good job, Antigone," said Mrs. Thompson. She called up the next person.

As Tig walked back to her seat, Kyra high-fived her. Tig couldn't believe Kyra was over it all, and so quickly. Regan was very good at what she did, whatever it was.

Later at lunch, Tig looked over to the Bots' table and found Regan's eyes. Tig shrugged and held up her palms in a "how did this happen?" manner, and Regan just smiled and gave a thumbs-up.

Thanking Regan had to wait until the next day because the only class she and Tig had together was math. Tig was waiting when Regan came into the room. "I totally flubbed that *Julius Caesar* speech in Mrs. Thompson's class yesterday," Regan said. She had Mrs. Thompson's English class a different period than Tig did. "I did the Brutus one. Which one did you do?"

"I did Caesar's," Tig said. "It was the shortest."

"Oh yeah, that cowards die bunches of times thing," Regan said. "I should've done that."

Tig couldn't wait through any more small talk. "How'd you do it?"

"After the whole 'as he was ambitious, I slew him' part, I went completely blank!"

"No, not the recitation," Tig said. "How'd you do it?"

"Do what?" Regan replied. "Oh, you mean that thing with Kyra? Piece of cake."

"What'd you say to her?"

"Nothing special. I just told her that I'd heard she was being a pain to you and to cut it out."

"That's it?"

"Pretty much."

Tig just stared at Regan for a moment.

"What?" Regan said.

"I don't get it," Tig said. "What makes you so powerful?"

Regan laughed. "I don't know. But it comes in handy sometimes."

"I'll say." Tig paused before continuing. "Thank you."

Regan smiled. "You're welcome."

"Is that all there is to it?"

"What do you mean? Was I supposed to say something other than 'you're welcome'?"

"No, I mean, is that all there is to this? I just say thank you and we're square? Don't I owe you something?"

Regan laughed again. "No charge. And tipping is not required."

"You know what I mean," said Tig. "Don't I have to do something for you now because you did something for me? I've got to be on the hook somehow."

"There's no hook," Regan said. "Sheesh. If anything, I probably owed you this one little favor for being such a jerk last year."

"I just don't get why you're being nice to me all of a sudden."

"Can't a person grow? Maybe I've become enlightened."

Tig grinned. "Maybe. If that's the case, I like Enlightened Regan way better than Jerk Regan."

"Join the club."

Will came in and sat down in his usual seat. "Olivia said it's all worked out with Kyra."

"Yeah," Tig said. "We may actually have a functioning band at the moment."

"So this Paris chick is playing bass now?" Will asked.

"Yep. She's good, too."

"I thought she was going to be rhythm guitar?" he said.

"That was the original plan, until we were down a bass player. Paris stepped up. We can manage without rhythm guitar for now."

"Who're you going to get for that?" said Will.

"Ugh!" Tig said. "Who knows? One problem at a time. I just got Kyra off my back. Let me revel in it for just a little while."

Will laughed. "Fair enough. You're pretty lucky that Robbie found Paris when she did."

Tig nodded. As the teacher began the day's lesson, Tig's mind stayed on what Will had just said. He was right: she was very lucky that Paris had come along. She was great on the bass and had been supercool about all the drama so far, even though she didn't have to be. It was now obvious to Tig why Robbie liked her so much. Maybe, in time, she and Paris would become close friends too.

And while Tig's mind was on the subject of friends, what about this new friendship with Regan?

There had to be a catch. Could there really be such a thing as Enlightened Regan?

Even though Regan had said Tig didn't owe her anything, Tig felt somehow obligated. Not so much in the sense of needing to pay off a debt, but more in the sense that one kindness deserved another.

"Hey," Tig said to Regan as the students filed out of the classroom. "Would you want to come by my house and watch band practice sometime? Just kind of hang out with us?"

Regan looked surprised. "Yeah," she said. "That'd be really cool. I'd love to."

"We usually do every Thursday starting around four," Tig said. "If for some reason that changes, I'll let you know. But feel free to drop by if you want."

"I'll do that," said Regan. "Oh, and I'll bring Haley and Sofia."

CHAPTER THIRTY-SIX

Tig's eyes got big. "Uh, uh . . . ," she stuttered.

"Kidding!" Regan said. "Bots can operate independently sometimes. Catch you later!"

As she watched Regan walk away, Tig stood, stunned. "They know we call them Bots?" she said out loud to no one in particular.

Chapter Thirty-Seven

"**Y**ou did *what?*"

Robbie was beside herself. Tig was glad she'd chosen to tell her the news over the phone instead of in person. At least this way, she had a safe distance.

"You invited a Bot—wait, not only a Bot, but the *head* Bot, the Queen of the Bots—to our practice? Have you lost your mind?"

"She's been really nice," Tig said.

"That just means she's up to something," Robbie said. "Have you forgotten last year? The relentless pursuit of our band's destruction that she engineered?"

"She's sorry about that."

"Oh, she's sorry, huh? Well, okay, then. Let's just forget the whole thing and invite her to the studio so she can gather intel for the next thing she does, and then I guess she can be sorry about that, too."

"Calm down," Tig said.

"You should've run it by us first," said Robbie.

"You're right," Tig said. "That would have been a courtesy. But I kind of did it spontaneously."

"You and your spontaneity," said Robbie.

"Look, she did us a real solid by getting Kyra off our backs."

"She certainly did," said Robbie. "Kind of makes you wonder, doesn't it?"

"Wonder what?"

"It wasn't so very long ago that Kyra went to Regan to try to help her take us down. Supposedly, according to Regan, who, by the way, is a highly unreliable source, Regan said no. Why? Because Regan is so noble now. Enlightened, did you say? And then, coincidentally, Regan helps us out yet again and makes Kyra behave.

And now Regan's our buddy? Doesn't that smell a little fishy to you? Like maybe this is all one big conspiracy? Like maybe the whole thing was planned from the beginning to get you to let your guard down?"

"Oh, come on."

"No, seriously. Think about it. This whole scenario hinges on two unlikely things: Regan being nice and Kyra suddenly realizing she was wrong and giving up her grudge."

Tig thought about that. Robbie did have a point. "Yeah, it is weird that Kyra would suddenly get over being mad, but think about it: if Regan told Kyra to paint herself purple and stand on top of a mountain, Kyra would run right to the paint store."

"And after that go pick up some rope and a grappling hook," said Robbie. "You've got that right. But you've got to remember: Regan is cunning. She may have told Kyra what to do from the beginning. Maybe she didn't turn down Kyra's offer to destroy the band. Maybe this whole thing has been planned out since that day, and all this is just to lull you into a false sense of security. Maybe they're in cahoots."

"Cahoots," Tig said. "That's a funny word."

"Focus, Ripley."

"I'm focused. I just don't think there's any reason to worry. I mean, what can Regan do at practice? Glue my hi-hat together? Break your guitar strings? Unplug the amps?"

"Of course not. She'd never do anything so simple. But she might try to get in our heads somehow. Throw off our confidence. Or stir up trouble between us the way Kyra tried to do."

"But Kyra failed," Tig said, feeling good about the fact that her friends hadn't turned on her despite Kyra's tactics.

"Kyra's a lightweight," Robbie said. "Regan's a pro."

"I'll be careful," Tig said. "And besides, you'll be there to keep an eye on her, so what can she really do? You don't think Regan could get away with anything with you there, do you?"

"I guess not," Robbie said. Tig was glad Robbie couldn't see her smiling, but she was quite pleased with herself. She knew Robbie would never admit that Regan could trick her, so this was the perfect tactic to get Robbie to relent.

"Then stop worrying," Tig said. "Who knows? Maybe Regan really has turned over a new leaf."

"If Regan turns over a leaf, there's probably a venomous snake under it," Robbie said. "I'm going into this with my eyes wide open, and if you're smart, you'll do the same."

"I hear you loud and clear," Tig said.

But when she hung up the phone, Tig shrugged off Robbie's warning. There was nothing in Tig's gut that told her to be on guard against Regan . . . at least not at band practice. Tig was certain there was nothing Regan could do at practice to cause trouble.

Chapter Thirty-Eight

Olivia and Claire were a bit surprised about the whole Regan-coming-to-practice thing, but not overly freaked out. In spite of what Regan had done last year, Olivia still clung to her belief that everyone was really good deep down, and Claire had actually been friends with Regan last year prior to Regan's forbidding her to sing with Pandora's Box. Claire acknowledged that Regan did have a side to her that Claire had liked, and she was willing to forgive last year's mistakes if Regan truly was trying to be a better person. Paris, as usual, was chill about anything and everything, and besides, she had heard about Regan and the Bots only secondhand from Robbie, so she hadn't really been involved in last year's drama.

Robbie, though, showed up at practice on high alert for anything Regan might try to pull. She was certain that Regan would, indeed, pull something.

"Maybe she's not coming after all," Tig said around 4:10.

"Good," said Robbie. But Tig thought Robbie seemed a little disappointed. She'd shown up ready to protect her territory, and now it looked as though there would be no one to protect it from.

"She may have had something else to do," said Claire. "Maybe we should just get on with practice."

The girls agreed and started "Signed, Sealed, Delivered." Claire was really loosening up and becoming more of a performer in addition to being an incredible singer. She even threw in a "yeah, yeah, yeah" while the girls sang the backup chorus. Paris was solid on bass; Robbie and Olivia, as always, handled their parts to perfection; and Tig nailed the phrasing on the toms during the chorus.

They were so into the song, they didn't even notice Regan standing in the doorway until she started clapping at the end. "Woo!" Regan said. "That was awesome! How do y'all do that?"

The girls stopped and said hello. "You want a drink or something?" Tig said, pointing to the mini-fridge her grandmother had recently bought for her at a garage sale.

"Sure, thanks," Regan said. She took a bottle of soda out of the fridge and sat down in the empty saucer chair in front of the band.

"By the way, this is Paris," Tig said. "Paris Nichols, Regan Hoffman."

"S'up, Regan?" Paris said.

"Good to meet you," Regan replied. "So, what else do y'all know how to play?"

The band struck up "For Your Love" and then "Twist and Shout." Tig was pleased that they had to restart both songs only once. "These are new ones for us," she explained to Regan.

"Don't apologize—you sound great!"

Regan's praise loosened the girls up, and once they were over their self-consciousness at playing in front of her, they were able to run through the entire set list. It sounded pretty good. Not as good as they would be in a couple more weeks, but still pretty good.

"Whew!" Tig said. "That's a wrap for today. Good job, ladies."

The girls clapped a little bit for themselves and high-fived.

"All of you are so good," Regan said. "Robbie, where'd you learn to play guitar like that?"

"Lessons," Robbie said flatly.

"Well, I'm sure that a lot of what you do can't be taught just in lessons. You're a natural rock star. The way you handle yourself while you're playing is really cool."

"Thanks," Robbie said. Tig could tell she didn't want to be sucked in by Regan's flattery, but how could she not enjoy it? Especially when it was all true.

"Ooh, my mom's pulling up," said Olivia. She took

a drink from the mini-fridge. "I'll take this one for the road. Later!" Claire's mom wasn't far behind. Soon it was just Robbie and Paris and Regan and Tig.

While Robbie and Paris played around with the guitar and bass, Tig showed Regan around her family's property. "We call this building 'the studio' because it's our practice area, but really it was a mother-in-law apartment built by the people who lived here before us."

"Cool," said Regan. "Show me your room?"

"Sure," said Tig.

In Tig's room, Regan went straight for the book-shelf. "Oh man! You still have these?"

Tig was embarrassed to see that Regan had picked up a collection of fairy books she'd read in elementary school. She'd gotten a cutesy little boxed set back in fourth grade that, for whatever reason, was still sitting on her shelf. Maybe it had been there so long, she didn't even really see it anymore, or maybe she had loved it so much, she just couldn't bear to part with it, even long after she'd stopped holding out hope that fairies were real. "I forgot that was even there," Tig said. "I liked those back when I was a kid."

"Oh, me too!" Regan said.

"You did?"

"Totally!" Regan said. "I even set my dollhouse out in my backyard, hoping that fairies would find it and move in and then be my friends."

"Really?" Tig was surprised that Regan would not only do something so silly but freely admit to it.

"Yeah!" Regan laughed. "I kind of forgot it was out there, and I left it for a few days, and it rained all over it. Pretty much ruined it. My mom was so mad!"

"No fairies moved in, I guess?"

"Unfortunately not." Regan smiled. "Hey, thanks again for letting me come over today to watch your practice. I really enjoyed it."

"We don't stink, then?"

"Not hardly," Regan said. "I'm sorry I gave y'all a hard time last year. You're really good."

"Well, last year, we did stink. But we're getting better. And our new bass player helps a lot. She's great."

"She seems nice," Regan said. "It's cool that you're all such good friends, too."

"It's the best," Tig agreed.

"How's everything with Olivia?" Regan asked. "Does she suspect that you like Will?"

"I never said I liked Will," Tig replied.

"Okay, okay," Regan said. "But I wouldn't blame you if you did. He's a little hottie."

Tig smiled. "He's Olivia's boyfriend."

"Right," Regan said. "Let's just keep repeating that: He's Olivia's boyfriend. He's Olivia's boyfriend. Oops! Guess what? Still a little hottie."

Tig laughed. "I'm not crushing on Will."

"I admire you for that," said Regan. "Especially when it's so obvious that he's crushing on you."

"You think so?" Tig asked—a little too quickly.

"I know so," Regan said. "It's painfully obvious. I can't believe Olivia doesn't see it."

Suddenly there was a knock on Tig's open door. Paris was making sure Tig and Regan noticed that she was standing there.

"Oh!" Tig said. "Hey, Paris."

"Hey," Paris replied. "Robbie left. My mom texted she was running a little late, so I just came in here to see what y'all were doing."

"Nothing," said Tig. "We're not doing anything." *Could you possibly sound any more guilty?* Tig said to herself.

"We were just talking about fairy books," Regan said, holding up the book collection to Paris. "Did you ever read these when you were little?"

"No," Paris said. "I must've missed those."

"Tig and I loved them," Regan said. "I was telling her about how I had put my dollhouse outside, and then it rained. . . ." Regan's phone buzzed. "My mom's outside," she said. "Thanks again for letting me watch practice. Catch y'all later."

"I'll walk you out," Tig said. Just before Regan got into her mom's car, Tig asked, "Do you think Paris heard us talking about Will?"

Regan grimaced. "I don't know. Tig, I'm sorry. I didn't know she was standing there. Honest."

"It's okay," Tig said. But she thought back to Robbie's warning that Regan would come to practice only to cause trouble. Had Regan intentionally brought up Will because she knew Paris would overhear them?

When Tig went back inside, Paris was looking at the fairy books. "These are cute," Paris said. "The little illustrations—"

"How long were you standing at the door?" Tig said. She hoped it didn't sound confrontational; she just couldn't stand not knowing.

"Just a little while," Paris said.

"Did you, um . . ."

Paris set the books down on Tig's desk. "Yeah," she said, "I heard y'all talking about Will."

Tig threw her head back, covered her face, and groaned.

"I'm not going to tell Olivia," Paris said. "Or Robbie. Or anyone else."

"I don't want to hurt Olivia," Tig said. "I've been trying to keep my distance from Will. Really, I have."

"I believe you," Paris said. "I know you wouldn't

hurt Olivia."

"I try my best not to even think about him," Tig said. "But then Olivia insisted he tutor me in algebra, and then there we were in the library after school, just the two of us, and his eyes were so blue, and . . . oh, Paris! I'm a terrible friend!"

"No, you're not," Paris said. "There's an old saying: 'The heart wants what it wants.' "

"What does it mean?"

"It means it's awfully hard to talk your heart out of something. Your heart makes up its own mind."

"I'm a middle-school girl," Tig said. "I'm supposed to be notoriously fickle. I'll be over this in a week or two, right?"

"You might if you weren't trying so hard," Paris said, smiling.

"But I have to try!" Tig said. "You want to hear something crazy?"

"Shoot."

"Last year Will liked me, and I kind of liked him, too. But I knew Olivia was crazy about him, so I pushed him her way. I'm pretty much the one who set them up."

"You want to hear another old saying?" Paris asked.

"Shoot," Tig said again.

" 'No good deed goes unpunished.' "

Chapter Thirty-Nine

The next day both Regan and Tig were early to algebra class. "How much did she hear?" Regan asked.

"I think pretty much all of it."

"Oh no. Tig, I'm so sorry."

Tig wondered if Regan really was sorry—or if Robbie had been right and Regan had shown up at practice for the specific purpose of causing trouble. Tig chose not to think about what Robbie had said. It was more comfortable to think that Regan wasn't out to get her. Why go borrowing drama when life seemed to offer plenty of it every time she turned around? "It's no big," Tig said. "Paris is cool. She's not going to go run her mouth about it."

"Whew," Regan said. "She is cool."

"It's funny," Tig said. "I didn't even like Paris at first."

"Why not?"

"I guess I was jealous. She's so pretty and she looks sixteen."

"Yeah, she does. But I guess if she's nice, you can overlook it."

"I think . . . Well, I don't *think*. I *know* what the real issue was. I was jealous because she and Robbie are so tight. I was being totally immature."

"But it's all in the past now," Regan said. "Now you're friends. I think it's awesome."

"What? Being friends with Paris?"

"The fact that you disliked her so much at first . . . and now you're friends."

"I guess that is pretty neat," said Tig.

"Kind of like with you and me," said Regan. "You hated me last year."

"What makes you think I like you now?" Tig said, but she smiled.

"Shut up!" said Regan. "You let me come to your house. We discussed fairy books! I told you my embarrassing fairy house story! That totally makes us friends now!"

"We'll see," Tig said, still smiling. "I don't want to rush to judgment on this."

"Maybe if you admit we're friends, Robbie won't hate me anymore either."

"Robbie doesn't hate you," Tig said. Regan gave her a look. Tig said, "Okay, she totally does. I'm sorry, but that's the truth."

Regan laughed. "I'll have to keep working on her, I guess. I can't blame her for not liking me after the way I acted last year. Anyway, I totally love your band!"

"You do?"

"Yeah! Pandora's Box rocks!"

"Thanks," said Tig. "We didn't always."

"Oh, trust me, I know," said Regan. "I saw the video last year. Over and over, actually."

Tig pushed Regan's shoulder. "*Saw?* You *engineered* the video last year."

"True," Regan said. "How did y'all go from that to this, anyway? That's a big jump from the video of you crashing and burning to what I saw yesterday. Did it just take you a year to get good?"

"Not exactly. A lot of it is practice and dedication," Tig said. "I think anyone who really has a passion for music and is willing to give it a real go and put in the work can learn pretty fast."

"Really?" Regan said. "You think I could learn how to play an instrument?"

"I'm sure you could," Tig said.

"Didn't you say Pandora's Box needed a rhythm guitarist? Isn't that why you said y'all brought Paris on to begin with?" Regan asked. "Since she's playing bass now, do you think I could try rhythm guitar?"

Everything seemed to stop for a moment. Tig became hyperaware of everything around her, like one of those scenes in the movies where the voice of the person speaking all of a sudden gets really loud and really slow, and their face comes into frame in an extreme close-up.

Tig felt as though the heavens had suddenly opened up and revealed a great truth to her.

"So that's what all this was about?" Tig asked.

"What all what was about?"

"Robbie warned me you were up to something," Tig said. "I actually almost believed you wanted to be my friend. But Robbie said you had an agenda. I just couldn't figure out what it could possibly be. But here it is."

"What agenda?" Regan said. "I just asked a simple question."

"Asking to join our band is not just asking a simple question," Tig said. " 'Can I borrow a pencil?' is a simple question. 'What time is it?' is a simple question. 'Can I join your band?' is most definitely not a simple question! It's a huge, life-changing question!"

"I didn't know it was that big a deal to just ask," Regan said. "Why are you getting so uptight?"

"I'm not uptight," Tig said. "I'm just opening

my eyes. I've got to hand it to you: you almost had me fooled. Well, the answer, Regan, is no. No, you may not join Pandora's Box. You tried everything to destroy it last year, and when you couldn't, when you saw that we were actually getting somewhere, you decided to worm your way in. What? You're not popular enough already? You couldn't stand for us to get some attention? You had to have that little bit of limelight too?"

"You're being ridiculous and you're really starting to tick me off," Regan said.

"Oh? Is that so?" Tig said. "Is that supposed to scare me? Guess what. I'm not scared of you. You threw everything you had at me last year, and I survived. What's more, Pandora's Box survived. There's nothing you can do to me now."

Just then Will walked in and sat down.

Tig gulped. As usual, she'd gotten angry and shot her mouth off again without thinking. Of course there was something Regan could do to Tig: she could tell Will and Olivia about Tig's crush. Sure, Tig could deny it, but would they believe her? And even if she did deny it and they bought it, once the suggestion was out there that Tig liked Will, she'd be under constant scrutiny, and they'd eventually see what she'd been trying so hard to hide. It was a bell she wouldn't be able to un-ring.

Regan must have known what Tig was thinking. Regan looked from Tig to Will and back to Tig.

Tig had to think fast.

She could either admit that Regan had her where she wanted her, or she could go down defiantly.

She chose defiance.

"Go ahead," Tig said. "Tell him. Tell Olivia. Tell the whole world if you want. I haven't done anything wrong."

Regan looked again at Will, then back to Tig.

"I said go ahead," said Tig. She tried to look tough. She crossed her arms in front of her so her hands wouldn't shake.

"You want me to tell Will?" Regan said.

Will turned around. "Tell me what?"

CHAPTER THIRTY-NINE

"Will," Regan said, "there's something you should know about your buddy Tig."

"Oh yeah?" Will said. "What's that?"

"She really, really likes . . . ," Regan began.

There was a pause.

"Really, really likes what?" Will asked. Tig could feel her face reddening. *Here it comes,* she thought, bracing for impact.

"Tig really, really likes . . . ," Regan said. She looked once more at Tig. "She really likes books about fairies."

Will scrunched his eyebrows. "Okay," he said. "Thanks for sharing." He turned back around and started unzipping his backpack.

Regan turned around too, putting her back to Tig.

What just happened? Tig wondered. *What does this all mean?*

Did it mean that Regan wasn't going to rat her out?

No way, Tig thought. *This is Regan Hoffman.* She thought of all the things Regan had done to her in seventh grade. Regan was no lightweight. When she wanted to take someone down, she brought her A game.

Regan must've had a good reason for waiting. Perhaps she wanted to prolong Tig's anxiety, to let her suffer with wondering when and how the secret would be revealed.

That was why Regan hadn't told Will, Tig decided. Regan was planning something horrifically spectacular.

Chapter Forty

Part of Tig wanted to tell the girls about it at lunch. But she couldn't. First of all, she didn't want to admit that Robbie had been right. For all Robbie's coolness, she wasn't above a good "I told you so." And second, Tig was afraid that if she told the girls about Regan, it would get around to the fact that Regan had something on Tig, and she certainly didn't want any of them asking what that might be. So Tig kept her mouth shut—so much so that everyone at the lunch table kept asking, "What's wrong with you?" She finally told them it was cramps just to get them to back off. What was one more white lie when she had become so adept at hiding her feelings for Will?

There were only about ten minutes left in the lunch period when Regan came over to their table.

"Hi, Regan," Kyra said. "Did you want to sit with us?"

Tig rolled her eyes. Of course Kyra never failed to hold out hope that she would finally be chosen to join the Bots.

"No, thanks," Regan said. "Tig, why don't you come sit at my table for a minute? We need to talk."

Tig started to tell Regan that she didn't take orders from her, but then, Regan hadn't really commanded her to join her at her table; she'd suggested it. And if Tig had balked, Robbie and the other girls would've known something was up. The wisest course of action seemed to be to go to Regan's table and hear her out, so that was what Tig decided to do.

Regan waved her hand at Sofia and Haley, who scurried over to the Pandora's Box table. Tig watched Kyra fall all over herself to make room for them while

Robbie looked on in horror. The other Bots at Regan's table turned their backs to Regan and Tig to give them some privacy. With all the noise in the lunchroom, Tig felt reasonably comfortable that no one would overhear the two of them.

"You owe me an apology," Regan said.

"For what?" Tig replied.

"For going psycho on me in algebra," Regan said. "I didn't do anything wrong. I didn't deserve to be treated like that."

"Do you really expect me to believe that you've been nice to me this year for no reason?" Tig asked.

"Of course there was a reason," Regan said.

"Aha!" Tig said. "So you admit it! Finally! Let's hear it. What's your game?"

"Okay," Regan said, "you're right. I have had a reason for being nice to you this year. And just as you suspected, it's the same reason I was out to get you last year."

Tig was a little taken aback that Regan was being so up-front about the whole thing. "So what is the reason?" she asked.

"Because I think you're cool," Regan said.

Tig sat in silence for a moment, then replied, "You what?"

"I think you're cool," Regan said. "I wanted to be your friend."

"Wait," Tig said. "Are you trying to tell me that you treated me like dirt last year because you wanted to be friends with me? That makes no sense at all."

"It didn't start out that way. I tried to be nice at first. But you were always so rude to me for no reason," Regan said. "Whenever I saw you in the halls, you'd scowl at me. Whenever I said anything in class, you'd roll your eyes."

"That's because you're a Bot," Tig said.

"That's exactly what I'm talking about!" Regan said. "You never tried to see who I really was. You just categorized me: *Bot*. You never tried to be nice to me."

"As if you needed me to be nice to you," Tig said. "Everybody in the whole school bows before you! You're the Queen Bot!"

"You're right," Regan said. "I'm the most popular girl in school. Pretty much everybody wants to be friends with me. But not you. It was like you thought you were too good for me. But I tried being nice to you. At first. Like that time I told you I liked your shirt."

"When did you do that?"

"The beginning of last year. I said, 'Nice shirt,' and you said, 'Whatever,' and looked at me like I'd just kicked your dog or something."

"I probably thought you were being sarcastic," Tig said.

"Well, I wasn't," said Regan.

Tig felt embarrassed. "I'm sorry," she said. "I don't know. . . . I guess I don't like to let my guard down."

"Have you noticed that you *never* let your guard down?" Regan asked. "You're like that thing in *Julius Caesar*. About dying a lot of little deaths instead of one big one. You're always so worried about something happening, you can't enjoy anything."

Tig thought about what Regan had said. She had

a point. When was the last time she wasn't worried about what might happen—with Regan and the Bots, or with Kyra, or with Claire, or with Robbie and Paris, or with Olivia and Will? "Okay, for argument's sake, let's say you're right. I expect the worst. But you're telling me that you were out to get me last year because I'd hurt your feelings?"

"It sounds pathetic when you say it that way," Regan said. "Let's just say I wanted to rattle you a little bit."

"Oh, you rattled me," Tig said. "You rattled me plenty."

"It never seemed that way," Regan said. "And then this year I thought maybe we could actually be friends. But of course, you were always on the lookout for some reason to hate me."

Tig sighed. "I just never wanted to be like Kyra—always chasing after the popular crowd. That just seems so lame."

"It *is* lame," said Regan. "It's kind of funny, I guess. I didn't want to be friends with Kyra because she tried so hard to be in my crowd, and I guess I wanted to be friends with you because you tried so hard *not* to be."

"Yeah," said Tig. "Kyra has been dying to be friends with you for years now."

"No, she hasn't. She's never been dying to be friends with me. She's been dying to be in my crowd. There's a big difference."

Tig nodded. "You're pretty perceptive for a Bot."

"Wow, thanks," said Regan.

"I'm just kidding," Tig said. "But look, this doesn't mean I'm going to become a Bot. You can't push me around and tell me what to do like you tried to do with Claire last year."

"I wasn't really trying to push Claire around," Regan said. "I really liked her. I just didn't want her to like you. I figured you'd turn her against me."

"I worried about the same thing with you."

"You won," Regan said. "Sofia and Haley sort of like me telling them what to do."

"And I'm sure you don't enjoy that at all," Tig said.

Regan smiled. "Maybe a little bit. Being the queen

does have its perks."

"I'm sorry," Tig said again. "For everything. I really am. But know this: I'm not putting you in the band."

"I understand," Regan said. "I'd probably be terrible anyway. And I guess I don't really deserve to be in your band. I did try to kill it a few times."

"That's true," Tig said. "But to be fair, you kinda helped us, too."

"Oh, you mean with the Kyra problem."

"Not just that. Remember last year when you told us we didn't look like rock stars at all?"

Regan winced. "Yeah, sorry about that."

"Don't be. It was actually helpful. We needed to hear that. That was the whole reason I changed my hair and we worked on costuming and stage choreography. If it hadn't been for you, we might have looked like total losers in UA's fake commercial."

"Oh. Well, you're welcome." Regan grinned. "See, I knew that all along, and that's why I did it. It was all part of my secret master plan to help you!"

"Yeah, right!" Tig laughed. "Tell you what. If you

really want to learn to play guitar, take some lessons. Try it out for a while. If you get any good in a few months and we're still looking, I'll talk to Robbie and the other girls about letting you audition."

"Come on," Regan said. "Like Robbie's ever going to give me a chance! Just go ahead and say no. Don't drag it out like that."

"You never know," said Tig. "Robbie's pretty open-minded once you get to know her. People can change their minds. If you'd told me last year that I'd be sitting here having this conversation with you today, I wouldn't have believed it. Would you?"

"No way," said Regan. "All right, then. Fair enough. I'll give guitar lessons a try. I might not even like it. Or I might get really good. Maybe I'll start my own band."

"If you do, here's a piece of advice," Tig said. "Don't let Haley be your lead singer."

Regan laughed. "Not in a million years!" she said.

Chapter Forty-One

The other girls were beside themselves wanting to know what had gone down between Tig and Regan at lunch. Kyra kept pestering Tig about whether the two of them were finally "in" with the Bots, and Robbie kept asking Tig if she'd lost her mind and why she would even consider sitting at the Bots table for any length of time. Tig promised both of them, and Olivia and Claire, a full explanation after school. But of course, Tig didn't trust Kyra with a full explanation of anything anymore, so she simply told her that she and Regan had buried the hatchet.

Kyra, who had hoped that Tig would be moving up the social ladder—and taking her along—was disappointed that the two of them wouldn't be sitting with the Bots at lunch. But she wasn't as disappointed as Tig had anticipated. Instead she recovered pretty quickly and wanted only to talk more about Milo. Same when Tig texted the relevant details about the conversation to Olivia, who quickly turned the conversation to Will. And, of course, his lack of crazy over her. Did Tig have any idea whom he might like? The answer to that increasingly tiresome question was still no.

Next, when talking to Robbie, Tig left out some of the details, such as Regan's asking to play rhythm guitar for Pandora's Box. No reason to get Robbie up in arms, Tig decided. Instead she told her about how Regan had pointed out Tig's tendency to worry too much. Robbie agreed that Regan had made a good point, but she still advised Tig to watch her back. If Regan hoped to win Robbie over, it would take a while.

Only Claire got the full lowdown about Regan and Tig's argument and resolution—well, minus the part about Regan's not telling Will that Tig secretly liked him. Everything else, though, Tig confided in Claire. Even the part about Regan's asking to play rhythm guitar.

"I figured it's best not to tell Robbie about that," Tig explained. "It would only upset her, and honestly, I don't think there's really any reason to be upset about it. Regan was cool when I told her no. No threats, nothing. She took it well."

"I understand," Claire said. "There's a difference between keeping secrets and not telling somebody something they probably don't need to know."

"And you know what?" Tig said. "I'm not going to worry about it. Regan was so right about all that. I worry way too much!"

"My mum says it gives you gray hair and wrinkles," Claire said. "That would be ever so attractive on a teenager!"

"Yeah, that's just what I need," said Tig. "Claire, do you think I'm doing the right thing by trusting Regan? Robbie still thinks I've lost it."

"Of course there's a chance Robbie is right," Claire said. "But hey, if she betrays you, she betrays you. You might as well be happy in the meantime. And who knows? Maybe the betrayal won't happen."

"I would never admit this to Robbie," Tig said, "but I actually kind of like Regan. More and more all the time."

"So did I, last year," Claire said. "You know, up until she forbade me to sing with the band. But she's apologized for that, and now that she's being so nice to you, too, I'm willing to give her another chance. She really can be a lot of fun."

"It's weird how different things are this year than last year," Tig said. "Things change so much every year. At the beginning of sixth grade, Kyra was my best friend. Had been since we were born. I used to tell her everything. Now everything's changed."

"Well, a lot has happened," Claire said. She didn't have to say any more. Tig knew she was talking about how Kyra had betrayed her secret about not liking Paris.

"It sure has," Tig said. "But it's not just Kyra and

me. Robbie and I aren't as close as we used to be—not that anything's wrong; it's just that she spends most of her free time with Paris now. And I guess that's cool. I mean, Paris is awesome. It's just different, that's all."

"On the upside," Claire said, "you and I barely knew each other last year, and look at us now. We can talk about anything."

"Yeah," Tig said. "You're right." There was a benefit to change after all. She remembered how much she liked Claire from the get-go last year, and how sad she'd been when Regan had tried to prevent them from being friends. And now here she was, confiding everything to Claire with full confidence that Claire would understand . . . and that she could be trusted. "And weirdest of all, who would've ever thought that I'd get to be friends with Regan Hoffman?"

Claire laughed. "Life is funny, isn't it?"

"Yes. But I'm not going to think too much about it. I'm just going to enjoy it, like you said. Hey, do you realize we have only one more week before the reunion gig?"

CHAPTER FORTY-ONE

"I can't believe I'm saying this, but I can hardly wait!" Claire said.

"You've got a little star quality happening, did you know that?" Tig said. "I think you're actually starting to like being up on stage."

"Like you said," Claire replied, "why worry when you can enjoy?"

Tig agreed. She was looking forward to the gig too—and she was determined not to worry about what could go wrong.

Chapter Forty-Two

At Thursday's practice, all the girls were on time, except for Kyra.

"I told her she could come late if she wanted," Tig explained. "She's performing just that one song, so all she has to do is run through 'Sweet Home Alabama' with us just to make sure she's fresh on it for the gig."

"That worked out nicely," Robbie said. "I'm glad she was cool about it."

"I think she's come to grips with the fact that she's not cut out to be a musician," Tig said.

"It doesn't hurt that she's so into this Milo guy,"

Olivia said. "Did you know that she's started watching foreign films? With subtitles and everything? Milo's a film buff."

"Whatever floats your boat," said Robbie. "Just float it away from the band."

Tig laughed. "That doesn't even make any sense."

"I think you get my meaning anyway."

Of course, they all knew what Robbie meant. Paris was a welcome change from Kyra on the bass. She practiced daily on her own and knew all the new songs for the gig. She was practically flawless.

After the girls had run through the set list once and were about to start the second run-through, Kyra showed up.

She wasn't alone.

"Everybody, this is Milo," Kyra said. A nice-looking dark-haired boy in a button-down shirt, jeans, and cowboy boots waved an awkward hello.

Tig was struck by the boots. Of all the things she'd heard about Milo—the brilliance in math, the philosophical conversations, the interest in foreign films—cowboy boots had just never entered her mind when she'd pictured him.

"Hi, Milo," Tig said. The other girls also said hello.

Milo didn't have much to say until after the girls, minus Paris and plus Kyra, played "Sweet Home Alabama." Then he had a lot to say.

A *lot* a lot.

"Southern rock isn't my preferred genre of music, of course . . . ," he began. "But one does have to admire this particular anthem, given its backstory."

"What backstory?" Tig asked. That was a mistake.

"Didn't you know?" Milo asked. "Of course you didn't. If you did, you wouldn't have asked." Milo laughed. Tig hoped he was laughing at his lame joke instead of at her ignorance. Milo continued. "You see, this song was in response to a tune called 'Southern Man' by the artist Neil Young. Young, one might argue, being an artist of more subtlety and nuance, of course . . . but nevertheless, the Lynyrd Skynyrd fellows apparently took umbrage at Young's critique of Southern society. Although I suppose that is actually debatable, as both the Skynyrd members and Young always maintained there was no real animosity between them. Nevertheless, this song was quite a clever riposte, don't you think?"

"I don't know," Tig said. "I don't know what a riposte is."

Milo laughed. Again, Tig didn't think he meant it insultingly. He seemed genuinely amused. "Forgive me!" he said. "Perhaps that's not a readily familiar word."

"I'm sure it's fine," said Kyra. "I bet Robbie knows what it means. Don't you, Robbie?"

"Well, yeah," Robbie said.

"Tell us," Kyra said.

"I don't want to show off," Robbie said. "You tell them, Milo."

Again, Milo laughed. "It's a fencing term," he said. "A quick thrust following a lunge. Do any of you fence?"

"Um, no," Tig said. "Do you?"

"Oh, indeed," Milo said. "I enjoy it immensely. I

must admit, though, I lack the hand-eye coordination and natural athletic prowess to be particularly good at it, but I do enjoy trying." He then launched into a ten-minute explanation of the art of fencing and its history.

When the girls thought they could take not one more second of Milo's tutorial, Robbie finally interrupted him. "That's very interesting. But we have to get back to practice."

"Yes, of course," Milo said. "You must forgive me. I tend to prattle on at times."

"You don't prattle," Kyra said. "We all thought that was really interesting, just like Robbie said!" Kyra's goo-goo eyes showed that she was being completely honest. Claire and Tig looked at each other and stifled a laugh.

"I think we're good on 'Sweet Home,'" Tig said, almost afraid to mention the song title again for fear that Milo would remember something else about its history that he hadn't shared. "Kyra, if you and Milo want to go in the house so you can talk, we understand.

CHAPTER FORTY-TWO

It's hard to have a conversation over our playing."

Kyra seized the opportunity to have Milo somewhat to herself, and took his arm as they left the studio. On her way out, she looked over her shoulder and gave the girls a big openmouthed smile as if to say, *Isn't he so great?* The girls smiled and nodded in response, giving the thumbs-up or "okay" hand signals.

Once Kyra and Milo were inside the house, Robbie finally spoke. "Girls, this proves it."

"Proves what?" Tig asked.

"It's true what they say. There really is someone for everyone."

The girls laughed. "When they first walked in, I was impressed," Olivia said. "He's kind of cute."

"I thought so too," said Claire.

"And then he started talking," Tig said. The girls giggled. "Sorry. That was unkind."

"But accurate," said Robbie.

"Now y'all see what I meant about Milo," Paris said. "He's nice and real smart, but sometimes I just don't believe his cornbread's all the way done."

"You have a lot of sayings about cornbread," Robbie said.

"Hey," Paris said. "Cornbread is life!"

"You're making me hungry," said Olivia.

Robbie smirked. "Shocker!"

"Back to Kyra," Claire said. "The important thing is that Milo likes her and she likes him. Did you see the way he looked at her? He's definitely smitten."

"I wish Will looked at me that way," Olivia said. "But he doesn't. Do y'all think he likes someone else?"

All the girls groaned.

"Well, do you?" Olivia asked.

" 'For Your Love,' from the top," Tig said, counting off with her sticks.

She kicked the bass drum with a little more intensity than on the last run-through, wondering what girls who didn't play the drums did to work out their frustrations.

Chapter Forty-Three

The night of BD's class reunion came.

The girls set up at the country club about an hour before the guests arrived.

"Swanky digs," Robbie said.

"Haven't you been here before?" Tig asked. Lots of people had wedding receptions at the country club. Tig's parents had dragged her to a few of them.

"Yeah," said Robbie. "But playing here feels different than showing up for a holiday party some professor friend of my parents is hosting. Performing here feels way cool."

"Performing anywhere feels pretty exciting to me," said Paris.

"Oh yeah!" said Tig. "I almost forgot that this is Paris's first gig!"

"I hope I don't mess y'all up," Paris said.

"Don't even worry about that," said Tig. "This is our first gig with an actual set list. Up until now, we've played one song and that's it. We did that video last year for the university's advertising students, and then we played a song at my aunt Kate's surprise party."

"And half a song at my birthday party," said Kyra.

"That doesn't count!" said Tig. "If we could all just stop talking about that, maybe I could forget it ever happened!"

The girls laughed.

"If we ever become famous, you know that video is going to go viral," said Robbie. "I'm so glad I wasn't there."

"If you had been, it wouldn't have gone down that way," Tig said. "But hey, water under the bridge, ladies. Water. Under. The. Bridge."

"Tig's right," said Olivia. "We don't need to be thinking about our past disaster. We need to have our minds on tonight and blowing the crowd away!"

"Yes," said Robbie. "By all means, let's blow away a bunch of octogenarians."

"They're not in their eighties yet," Tig said.

"Close enough," said Robbie.

"I'm just glad to have an audience at all," said Claire.

"Look at Shy Girl over here," said Robbie. "Life outside the shell kind of rocks, huh?"

Claire blushed. "What can I say? I'm loosening up."

"You got that right," said Tig. She surveyed their stage outfits. She wore shorts and an eyelet top with wedges, but she had to make sure the heels weren't so high that she couldn't work the hi-hat and bass pedals. Claire wore a simple, long, black dress with white sneakers. Olivia had chosen a demure pink top with a lace collar and little bow but paired it with a sequined skirt. Robbie's emerald-green silk jacket was paired with large dangling leather-and-metal earrings.

Paris kept her clothes simple with a white, sleeveless shirt and jeans, keeping the focus on her high, tight ponytail and bright purple and blue eye shadow. Kyra, apparently deciding to make her last time onstage memorable, wore an embroidered strapless dress.

"Y'all, this is going to be a great night. Claire's over her stage fright, Olivia's got great keyboard arrangements, Robbie's . . . well, still Robbie . . . and Paris, I've got to hand it to you, you are solid on the bass. You've worked really hard, and it's paid off. We are a pretty decent band, if I do say so myself."

"Don't forget our fearless leader and kick-butt drummer," said Robbie.

Tig smiled and took a bow. Kyra cleared her throat.

"Oh, and let's not forget our special guest performer," Tig said. "Kyra . . . way to play 'Sweet Home Alabama.' "

Kyra laughed. "Hey, it's only taken me over a year to get it down." Then she got serious. "But thanks for letting me play tonight. I know you kind of had no choice, but after the way I acted, I'm lucky y'all are even speaking to me. I want you all to know I realize now that I'm not a good bass player, and you were right to have Paris replace me."

Tig suddenly felt guilty. "Kyra," she said, "there's something we should tell you."

"What?" asked Kyra.

"I know you're only fine with this because Regan told you to be," Tig said. "But you should know that Regan talked to you about it because she was trying to do me a favor."

"I know that," said Kyra.

"You do?" asked Tig.

"Yeah," said Kyra. "Trust me: I felt like an idiot for the way I'd acted before Regan said a word to me. I would've apologized anyway . . . eventually."

"There's one other thing," said Tig.

"If it's about Milo, I know about that, too," said Kyra.

"You do?" said Paris.

"Of course," said Kyra. "Right after I act like a jerk at band practice, you introduce me to this totally hot guy? I knew you were trying to get my mind off my parents' divorce . . . and the band."

"And you're not mad?" asked Claire.

"Mad?" said Kyra. "If I'd known that all I had to do to be set up with a guy like Milo was be a brat, I'd have done it a long time ago! I should be a brat more often!"

"You're sure you're not mad?" Tig asked.

"No way!" said Kyra. "And Milo's been great for me. He understood how I felt about not being good at music because he got cut from the football team. But look how amazing he is at so many other things! He kind of made me realize that not being talented at one thing doesn't mean I'm worthless. And seriously, I have been so happy not having to think about the bass! I don't know how y'all do it. Playing music is hard. You all seem to enjoy it so much, but I'm just not cut out for it. It felt like brain surgery. All those different notes and keys and chords . . . ugh! You can have it!"

"The band's not the same without you, though," Robbie said. Everyone stared at her in disbelief. "It's way better now." Robbie burst out laughing, and Kyra joined her.

"Shut up!" Kyra said, still laughing.

Soon the guests began to arrive, and before the girls knew it, BD was at Claire's mic, introducing them. "Ladies and gentlemen, please welcome Pandora's Box!" The crowd responded with applause and cheers as the girls launched into "Signed, Sealed, Delivered."

It was adorable, really, watching all those old people try to dance. Tig kept waiting for one of them to twist wrong and then scream out, *Ahhh! My lumbago!*, and for the paramedics to have to be called, but it never happened. Tig wasn't really sure what lumbago actually was, but she'd heard the word in commercials for old people's medicines, and figured it had something to do with aging.

One of the couples really knew how to cut a rug. Tig wasn't sure what their dances were called, but the couple knew all the steps and put on a real show, especially on "Twist and Shout." They did the sort of dance moves that had long since fallen out of fashion, with the partners matching each other step for step and the man twirling the lady every so often. Tig sort of wished she could dance like that; it looked fun.

When they got to "Sweet Home Alabama" and Kyra subbed in for Paris, Norman Allen shouted, "That's my girl!" That song, along with all the others, was flawless. The girls kept getting more and more relaxed and playing even better with each song until before they knew it, their hour was up.

After their set was over, the girls hung around and had a glass of punch while taking in the scene. Old records played over the sound system, and the reunion crowd continued to dance. BD and Mimi sat at the table with Tig and the girls. There was a bar, and some of the old people were getting a little tipsy. It was kind of hilarious. One of the old men was making the rounds with the ladies, asking them to dance and putting his arm around them.

"Who's that old guy who keeps macking on the women?" Tig asked her grandparents.

After Tig had defined the word *macking*, BD replied, "Oh, that's Wayne Collins. He's a widower. He's been chasing the widows around all weekend. He hasn't changed a bit. Girl crazy in high school, too."

Tig wondered if people really stayed the same when they got older. She tried to picture herself and her friends. Would Robbie have a purple streak in her gray hair? Would Kyra still be following Regan and the Bots around? Would the Pandora's Box girls still play together in a band?

As Tig was trying to picture herself on the drums as an old lady, Norman Allen approached their table. "Why, young'un, you've grown like a weed since I last saw you!" he said to Tig. Tig smiled politely as he told her what height she had been at their last encounter a few years ago. "Good thing you look like your grandmother instead of this old guy," he said. BD laughed good-naturedly and agreed with him, but Tig thought it was kind of rude.

"I bet you didn't know that your grandmother and I were sweethearts back in high school," Mr. Allen said.

Tig pretended to be surprised. "Can't say that I did."

"Yes," he said. He got closer, and Tig could smell

that he had taken advantage of the bar. "She was pretty crazy about me, but so was this other one." He squared his shoulders proudly and gestured toward the area where his wife was sitting. "Had to cut one of 'em loose. Ain't that right, Donna?" he said to Tig's grandmother.

"Of course, Norman," she said. She and Tig's grandfather looked at each other and grinned.

Mr. Allen laughed, slapped BD on the back, and stumbled back over to his wife, who, in Tig's mind, seemed way too good for him.

"Why'd you let him do that, Mimi?" Tig asked. "That's not how it happened at all! You dumped him!"

Mimi waved her hand. "For heaven's sake, that was fifty-something years ago. What difference does it make?"

"But it's not true!" Tig said.

"Oh, honey, if Norman needs to believe all that to keep his dignity, who am I to take that away from him?"

Tig let her grandmother's words sink in. Was that what it was like to be old? To not care anymore about what other people thought and said? To have the confidence to live your own life without feeling the need to change other people or set them straight?

Tig decided that, gray hair and wrinkles and lumbago aside, getting old must not be all that bad.

Chapter Forty-Four

"I was kind of expecting cash, but this is better," Robbie said, holding up the check that night at Tig's house.

"Three hundred and twenty-five dollars," Tig said. "I'm glad it's a check too. That way we can make color copies of it and frame them or put them in scrapbooks or something."

"You have a scrapbook?" Claire asked.

"No," Tig said. "But I might start one, just for this."

"That was nice of them to give us a tip," said Robbie.

"I think Kyra would agree with that," said Claire. The girls had decided to give Kyra the extra twenty-five dollars, and she hadn't refused. Even so, Kyra hadn't come along with the rest of the girls to put equipment away at the studio. She'd gone home right after the gig so she could Internet chat with Milo.

"Are you sure you guys don't want to stay over?" Tig asked.

"I appreciate the offer," Paris said, "but I've got that 4-H show bright and early tomorrow morning. I think Betsy has a good chance at a blue ribbon. And Lola and Baby might place too. They're all clipped, with a pretty little swish at the tail, and I trimmed their hooves yesterday."

"You trimmed their hooves without me?" Robbie said.

Robbie's sarcasm wasn't lost on Paris. "I couldn't wait forever," she replied. She lightly kicked Robbie behind one knee to throw her off-balance.

"Just think: my first goat competition," said Robbie. "I feel so rural." Robbie had also bowed out of Tig's invitation earlier because she'd already made plans to sleep over at Paris's and attend the 4-H event the next day.

"Promise me you'll take pictures," Tig said to Paris.

"Of Betsy, Lola, and Baby?"

"Sure, them, too, if you want," said Tig. "But I meant of Robbie. I just can't picture her at a goat show."

"I am multifaceted beyond your wildest dreams, Ripley," Robbie said.

"I don't doubt it."

Paris's mom arrived and collected the two girls plus Olivia. They were dropping her off at her house on their way because she had a tennis match the next morning.

"Bye," Tig and Claire called as their three friends drove away.

"Guess it's just you and me," Tig said.

"I know," Claire replied. "It's a bit odd, isn't it? Do you think we'll be able to make conversation?"

Tig laughed. "I think we can handle it."

It turned out that the two of them had plenty to

talk about. So much so that they stayed up until after midnight just chatting and laughing. The funny part was, when they finally woke up around ten the next morning, neither of them could remember a thing they'd talked about. It had all just been so random and fun and easy. When Claire's mother picked her up just before lunch, Tig felt a little lost on her own. She couldn't remember when she'd had such a fun night.

For the first time since she could remember, Tig had absolutely no worries. Everything was finally falling into place. It felt awesome.

The feeling lasted for about another hour before her phone rang.

She looked at the screen.

It was Will.

Chapter Forty-Five

"**H**ello?" Tig said.

"Hey," Will said.

"Hey."

"What are you doing?"

"Nothing. Claire just left a little while ago. She spent the night last night."

"Oh. Did y'all have fun?"

"Yeah."

"How was the gig?"

"Good."

A long pause.

"I need to talk to you," Will said. Something in his voice sounded ominous.

"Okay," Tig said. "Go ahead."

"I need to talk to you in person."

"Like, at school Monday?"

"No. I need to talk to you . . . alone."

Tig's stomach dropped. "Is something wrong?"

"No," Will said. "I mean, yes. I mean . . . I don't know. Sort of."

"Can't you just tell me over the phone?"

"I don't think so," Will said. "My older brother has a car. I could get him to drive me over to your house if that's okay."

A dozen different thoughts went through Tig's head. What would Olivia think about Will coming to her house to talk to her? Would Tig's parents allow a boy to come over to see her? What did he want to talk about that couldn't be said over the phone?

"I don't know. I'd have to ask my folks if it's all right with them."

"I understand. Can you ask them and call me back?"

"Okay," Tig said. She hung up with Will and went to find her mom.

Her dad was in the laundry room, replacing a fuse in the dryer. "Dad," Tig said, "have you seen Mom?"

"Yes," he replied. "She's about five-foot-five, brown hair . . ."

Tig didn't laugh. "Dad, do you know where she is?"

"She's at the grocery store. Probably be back in about another hour. What's the matter?"

Tig sighed. It would've been awkward enough to talk to her mom about this, but her dad? Of all the luck!

"Is it okay if my friend Will comes over for a little while?"

"Your friend Will?" her dad asked.

"Yes, sir."

"Will sounds like a boy's name. Is your friend Will a boy?"

"Dad, you know Will. He played guitar for the band last year at Kyra's birthday party. He came over here for practice a bunch of times."

"Ah yes," her dad said. "That Will. But you're telling me he wants to come over here by himself, without your bandmates around?"

"Yes, sir."

"Hmmm," said her dad. "What will the three of us be talking about?"

"Dad," Tig said, losing her patience.

"Okay, okay," Mr. Ripley said. "I guess he can come over for a little while. But I'm not sure I like this."

I'm not sure I do either, Tig thought.

"And just so this fellow knows . . ." Tig's dad made a V with his index and middle fingers and pointed at his eyes, then at Tig, to mean, *I'll be watching*.

Tig called Will back. "You can come over," she said. She thought of her dad's V signal. "But I think maybe we should just sit outside on the studio steps."

"Good enough," said Will. "I'll be there in twenty."

Chapter Forty-Six

Tig realized her hair was a mess, so she ran a flat iron along the front and changed out of her sweats and XL T-shirt from youth group and into a decent tee and jeans. It occurred to her, as she was getting dressed, that she was fixing up to meet her friend's boyfriend. The thought unsettled her, so she pushed it out of her mind and chalked up her interest in her appearance to mere common courtesy.

When she heard Will's brother's car pull into the gravel driveway, she took one last quick look in the mirror, smoothed her hair with her hand, and went outside.

"Hey," she said as Will's brother drove away.

"Hey," Will said. "You look pretty."

Tig made a face. "Oh, I just rolled out of bed a little while ago."

"You want to sit?" Will asked, gesturing to the studio steps.

"Sure."

They walked to the steps together and sat down. Tig thought she saw the blinds in the living room move. She wondered if her dad really was spying on them or if it was just a curious, giggly younger sib.

"So, what's up?" Tig asked. "What's this all about?"

"I think I'm going to have to break up with Olivia," Will said.

"Will! You can't!" Tig said. "She'll be heartbroken!"

"I've thought of that," Will said. "I feel like a real jerk about it. I like Olivia. Really, I do. She's a sweet girl, and she's been really nice to me. But I don't *like* her like her. I've tried, Tig. I just don't. I can't."

"Why can't you?"

"You know why," Will said. "Do you want me to say it?"

"No," Tig said. "Don't say it. Because if you say it, then I'll know. And if I know, and I don't tell Olivia, then I'm hiding something from her. And that's not what friends do."

"What do friends do, Tig?" Will asked. "Do they push aside their own feelings so their friends don't get hurt?"

"I don't know," Tig said. "Maybe."

"You ought to know."

"What's that supposed to mean?"

"It means that this whole thing is your fault in the first place."

"My fault?!" Tig said.

"Yes, your fault," said Will. "I was trying to tell you last year . . . the thing you don't want me to tell you . . . and you stopped me and told me I should like Olivia. So I tried. And now I'm in this mess."

Tig didn't know which of her feelings to listen to first. It made her angry that Will was blaming her for his problems; then it made her feel bad because she knew he had a point. Plus, on the one hand, she felt both excited and relieved that Will still liked her, but on the other, she felt disloyal to Olivia. "Olivia is a great girl," Tig said. "A lot of guys would like to be in your 'mess,' as you call it."

"You know what I mean," Will said. "Olivia is great. She's perfect for some other guy. Any other guy who's not already crazy about you!" He blurted it out so fast that his mouth fell open afterward, as though he might try to push the words back inside.

Tig silently sat there, stunned. Not only had Will said the words she'd told him not to say, he'd even used the phrase *crazy about*. She couldn't help but think of all the times Olivia had used that exact phrase herself when talking about Will, wishing he were crazy about her. Tig thought of how betrayed Olivia would feel if she had heard Will say those words to her.

"I wasn't supposed to say it out loud," Will said. "I'm sorry."

Tig buried her face in her hands. "This is terrible."

"Which part?"

"All of it!"

"Even the part about how much I like you? How I can't stop thinking about you, no matter how hard I try?"

Tig looked up at Will. Their eyes locked. She couldn't speak.

"Tell me you don't feel that way about me, and I'll never bring it up again," Will said.

Tig put her head back in her hands. "I can't."

"I knew it," Will said. "I knew it."

Tig looked back up at him. "But what good does any of it do? I can't be your girlfriend. It would kill Olivia. And now we have this big thing out there between us, and we have to keep it a secret, which means we're lying."

"Keeping something to yourself isn't necessarily lying," Will said. "You don't say every single thought you have out loud, do you?"

"No, that's Robbie."

Will smiled. "The point is, some things are private.

They're no one else's business."

"Let's say you're right," Tig said. "What good does it do us if we like each other and we can't let anyone know?"

"I don't know," Will said. "I guess I could feel happy inside just knowing you felt the same way."

Will tried to take Tig's hand, but she pulled it away. "I can't," Tig said. "I can't be the reason you break up with Olivia."

"I'm breaking up with Olivia regardless," said Will. "It's not fair to her to drag this out any longer."

Tig nodded. "I guess you're right. You'll be nice about it, though? Let her down easy?"

"You're saying I should ditch my original plan of screaming at her and calling her names?"

Tig smiled. Of course Will would be nice about it. He was nice about everything.

"Just, whatever you do, don't tell her you like someone else," Tig said. "She couldn't handle it."

"Of course I wouldn't do that," said Will. "I like Olivia as a person. I wouldn't hurt her on purpose.

Maybe after some time has passed, we can all be friends again, and maybe she won't even mind if you and I like each other."

"Sure," Tig said. "And as long as you're having this wonderful dream, can I also be the best drummer in the history of rock? And Led Zeppelin re-forms and asks me to take John Bonham's place?"

Chapter Forty-Seven

Olivia called Tig the next afternoon, crying.

"What's wrong?" Tig asked, as if she didn't already know.

"Will," Olivia said. She blurted out other words, but Tig couldn't understand any of them. Olivia was too beside herself.

"Calm down," Tig said. "I'm sure it can't be that bad."

"Will broke up with me," Olivia said, this time more clearly.

"Oh," Tig said. "I'm sorry, Olivia." *If only you knew*

just how sorry, Tig thought.

"Did he say why?" It was Claire's voice. Tig hadn't realized it was a conference call.

Olivia cried a little more, then gathered herself enough to say, "He said it wasn't me; it was him. What is that supposed to mean?" Olivia cried still more. "Of course it's me! He doesn't like me. Why doesn't he like me? What's wrong with me?"

"Nothing is wrong with you, Olivia," Claire said. "Boys can just be such losers sometimes!"

Tig started to defend Will, to insist that not having feelings for someone didn't make him a loser, but she feared that she might give herself away. The part she was expected to play here was the sympathizing shoulder to cry on, who insists that the ex wasn't good enough for her brokenhearted friend in the first place. But Tig couldn't in good conscience say anything bad about Will, so she just kept saying she was sorry.

No one lectured Olivia about finding her identity outside of a relationship, so Tig surmised that Robbie hadn't been included in the call. As Olivia told her sad story and obsessed over what she'd done wrong, Tig and Claire just listened and assured her she was a wonderful person and that Will was really missing out.

"Do you need us to come over?" Claire asked.

"No," Olivia said, sniffling. "I'll be all right."

"Of course you will," said Claire. "And if you need to talk any more, Tig and I are here for you."

Tig hoped Olivia wouldn't feel the need to take Claire up on that offer. She wasn't sure she could handle any more; she already felt guilty enough.

Monday at school was beyond awkward. Olivia walked around like someone who'd lost all hope and whose only wish left in life was to be run over by a bus. When Will came into the gym that morning, he furtively glanced at the spot where they all usually sat, then went to sit with a group of boys from the school band. "He barely even looked at me!" Olivia said, starting to well up again. "And he isn't sitting with us anymore!"

"Olivia, get ahold of yourself," Robbie said. "What was he supposed to do, stare at you? Then come and sit down like nothing ever happened? He's probably scared to death that we're going to yell at him."

"Maybe we *should* give him a piece of our minds," Claire said. "Look at the way he's hurt poor Liv!"

"Look, I don't mean to sound unsympathetic," said Robbie. "But what's the guy supposed to have done, proposed marriage? We are, after all, in middle school. Breakups happen every day. Olivia, you've got to snap out of it!"

Olivia started to cry.

"Now look what you've done," said Claire, patting Olivia as she cried.

"Didn't I warn her not to become a boyfriend girl?" Robbie said to Tig. "This is what happens to boyfriend girls!"

"Olivia," said Tig, "Robbie didn't mean to upset you. She just wants you to feel better. Isn't that right, Robbie?"

Robbie softened. "Of course. I just hate to see you

make a muffin out of a molehole, as Paris would say."

Paris!

Tig hadn't even thought about Paris!

Paris knew everything!

What if, when Paris found out about the breakup, she told Olivia what she'd overheard Tig and Regan saying about Will? Tig felt sick.

She'd have to call Paris that afternoon and assure her she'd had nothing to do with the breakup. So far, Paris hadn't said a word to anyone about Tig and Will liking each other. Maybe she would continue to keep the info to herself. If Olivia was this upset now, Tig could only imagine how much more upset she'd be if she knew Will's true feelings.

Kyra came into the gym, practically bouncing. She had a big smile on her face. "Hey! Guess what," she said. Then she saw Olivia, and her smile immediately faded. "What happened?"

"Will broke up with her," Tig said. Upon hearing it said out loud, Olivia began crying harder.

"Oh, Olivia," Kyra said. "I'm so sorry! Are you all

right?"

"Does she look all right?" Robbie said. "Seriously, Liv, you've got to buck up. I'd die before I'd let some boy know he'd made me cry. Don't let him see you like this!"

But Olivia was on a jag and couldn't be stopped.

"That's terrible," Kyra said. "I can only imagine how you must feel. Breakups can be very traumatic." Tig couldn't help but roll her eyes. Kyra'd had her first boyfriend for only a few weeks, and suddenly she was a relationship expert. Kyra turned her attention back to Tig. "Now I feel kind of bad for being so happy this morning."

"You've got some happy to share?" Tig said. "By all means, share it. We could use some around here."

Kyra switched gears back into excited mode. "What would you girls say if I told you I'd gotten Pandora's Box an audition?"

"Well," said Robbie, "first I'd say, 'An audition for what?' and next I'd say, 'What's in it for you?' Are you trying to play bass for us again?"

"You're so cynical," said Kyra. "I already told you: I'm over wanting to play in the band."

"Just so long as we understand each other," Robbie said. "So what *is* in it for you?"

"Nothing," said Kyra. "I was just trying to be a good friend. Excuse me for being nice!"

"What's the audition for, Kyra?" Tig asked.

Kyra got a big smile again. "You're not going to believe it! West Alabama . . . Academy . . . *prom!*"

All the girls gasped. Even Olivia stopped crying and looked excited. Even Robbie seemed impressed.

"Wait a minute," Robbie said. "You're telling me that you got us an audition to play West Al's prom? No way. That's one of the sweetest gigs in town."

"I know," said Kyra. "But I'm awesome."

"How?" Tig asked. "How'd you get us an audition?"

"My next-door neighbor Mrs. Marquez is a teacher there," Kyra said. "She's also the senior-class sponsor. It was my mom's weekend to be at the house with me, so . . ."

"Wait . . . what?" Robbie asked.

"It's a custody arrangement thing until their divorce case goes to court," Tig explained. "Her parents take turns living in the house with her until the settlement is final."

"Sheesh," Robbie said. "That's rough."

Kyra continued. "So Mom was trimming the sasanquas this weekend, and Mrs. Marquez happened to be in her yard and—"

"What's a sasanqua?" Robbie asked.

Kyra scoffed. "It's a camellia. Don't you know anything?"

"Can we focus, please?" Tig said.

"Anyway," Kyra continued, "they were talking about how Mrs. Marquez was planning the prom, so I popped over and joined in the conversation. I said Pandora's Box was the hottest new band in town and that I had connections and might be able to persuade them to consider auditioning."

"But we're not the hottest new band in town," Tig said. "We've had only one real gig, and that was for senior citizens."

"It's called buzz," Kyra said. "Before you can actually *become* the hottest new band in town, someone has to start *saying* you're the hottest new band in town!"

"She's not wrong," said Robbie. "Buzz is a big deal."

"So is having a full set list," said Tig. "The West Al prom is probably a three-hour show."

"Four, actually," said Kyra. "But you really just play three. Two hours, an hour break, and then the last hour."

"We've got maybe an hour's worth of songs, if we push it," said Tig. "What do we do for the extra two hours? Hum?"

"I thought for three grand, you might be able to figure something out," said Kyra.

"Three grand?" said Robbie. "Shut up!"

"The academy doesn't do anything halfway," Kyra said. "They get most of their bands through the special events companies out of Atlanta or Montgomery or Birmingham. Three thousand is the minimum going rate these days."

"That's a thousand dollars an hour!" said Tig.

"Yeah," Kyra said, feigning a sad face. "It's just too bad you don't have three hours' worth of songs."

"For a thousand bucks an hour," Tig said, "we'll figure something out."

Chapter Forty-Eight

The first bell had rung before the girls could discuss the prom audition further, but Tig could barely concentrate all morning. Three thousand dollars! The West Al Academy prom! Did she dare dream it could really happen?

"I still can't believe you got us an audition," Tig said to Kyra at lunch.

"I can't wait to tell Paris," Robbie said. "Curses on the school's cell phone ban! I'll have to wait until I get home."

"You think she'll want to do it?" Claire asked.

"Of course!" said Robbie. "Six hundred dollars buys a lot of livestock."

"Does it?" Claire asked. "How expensive is livestock?"

"I don't know, Claire," Robbie said with a sigh. "I was just saying . . . I think Paris would do the gig just for the fun of it, but the money makes it even better."

"We need to start strategizing for your audition," Kyra said.

"Important question," said Robbie. "When is this big audition, anyway?"

"You have two weeks to prepare," Kyra said. "Luckily my mom trimmed the sasanquas when she did, or I might not have found out about the audition date in time for you to prep."

"Two weeks!" Robbie said. "That's not enough time to get down a three-hour set list!"

"We don't have to know all the songs by then," said Tig. "We'll just have to tell them what we'll be able to deliver. We can get the list together by then. An audition would just be a couple of songs."

"Right," said Claire. "All we'd have to do is select what we think we can master by the actual prom night. If we get the job, then we get to work on making sure we can deliver what we promised."

"This is such a rush!" said Tig. "I mean, a huge challenge for the entire band, yes . . . but how exciting! Of course we'll all have to give one hundred and ten percent, but we can do that!"

"I don't think I can," Olivia said. Until she'd finally spoken up, Tig hadn't even noticed how quiet Olivia had been about the whole thing. Tig had been too pumped to pay attention.

"What?" Tig said. "What do you mean you can't? Of course you can!"

"I just don't have it in me right now," Olivia said. "I'm too depressed. Y'all can do the audition . . . and the gig . . . without me."

"Oh no, you don't!" said Robbie. "If this were about a busy tennis schedule, that would be one thing. But no way are we going to let you miss a chance like this so you can sit around and pine away for a boy!

Nobody in this band is turning into a boyfriend girl on my watch!"

"Oh no! Not the 'boyfriend girl' lecture again!" Kyra groaned. She got up and went to buy a carton of milk.

"Robbie's right, though," said Tig. "Olivia, you can't miss this opportunity. And we wouldn't feel right playing without you."

"I think it would be good for you, Olivia," said Claire. "This will give you something to focus on and take your mind off . . ." Claire stopped. Tig supposed she was afraid to even say Will's name for fear of setting Olivia off again.

"Nothing can take my mind off Will," Olivia said.

"You won't know until you try," said Robbie. "And just think! Three thousand dollars, divided by five, is six hundred bucks! Just think of the retail therapy you can afford with that kind of dough!"

Olivia didn't say anything for a moment. Then she replied, "Well, now that you mention it, there is this leather purse that might ease my pain a little bit. But only a little." Olivia mustered a slight smile.

"That's my girl!" Robbie said. "See there? You're on your way back already!"

"Um, guys," Tig said. "I think maybe Robbie miscalculated."

"No, I didn't. Three thousand divided by five is six hundred."

Tig thought back to the joke her parents had made when BD had gotten them the class reunion gig—about an agent's fee. "What's fifteen percent of three thousand?"

Robbie looked at the ceiling to calculate. "Four hundred fifty. Why?"

"I think we owe Kyra an agent's fee," Tig said. "Assuming we get the job, which is a big assumption."

"Are you actually suggesting we toss four hundred fifty bucks at Kyra just for talking to her neighbor over the sasanquas?" Robbie said. "That cuts each of our pay down to only five hundred ten dollars!"

"That's five hundred ten dollars we wouldn't have if it weren't for Kyra," Tig said.

"True," Claire said. "And I don't want to be greedy, but maybe we should take some time to think about this and then vote. I appreciate what Kyra's done, but as Robbie said, four hundred fifty dollars is quite a bit of money for simply speaking to her neighbor."

"I agree with Claire," Olivia said. "We need to think about it. I don't think Kyra expects to be paid. I think she just did it to be nice. And after the way she acted at the studio that day, maybe she owes us one anyway."

"We'll think it over, then," Tig said. "Here she comes."

"That line is ridiculous," Kyra said, taking her seat. "I thought lunch would be over before I paid for my milk! Anyway, back to your set list."

"For high schoolers, we're going to have to learn a lot of current pop," Robbie said. "Which, to be clear, pains me."

"Selling out already, huh?" Tig said.

"You bet," said Robbie. "I can be bought."

"Actually," said Kyra, "I wouldn't go that route. West

Al's prom is different from other proms. It's not just the students; their parents and the faculty all come too."

"What?" Tig said. "How weird is that?"

"Not that weird when you think about it," Kyra said. "Their school is small, and a lot of them have gone there since preschool. The teachers there have taught some families for a few generations. They're tight-knit. They do this thing called the senior lead-out, where they call each senior's name and they kind of parade in front of everyone with their date, and everybody claps for them. It's kind of a thing for the parents to be there to witness the big moment."

"How do you know all this?" Tig asked.

"Just took some time to ask Mrs. Marquez the right questions, I guess," Kyra said. "Anyway, if you want to get hired, I'm thinking you appeal to the whole crowd, not just the students. Yeah, you need a few contemporary songs, but you're also going to need to cover several decades and all the styles: slow songs for slow dances, upbeat numbers, classics everybody knows, and probably some Motown because it's easy to dance to and everybody knows it and likes it."

"We've already got 'Signed, Sealed, Delivered' from the reunion!" Tig said.

"Also, you need something for the ones who aren't that good at dancing. Something to get full crowd participation. You've got to bring everybody in. Do something they can all jump around to, or something that gets everybody's hands in the air or whatever. And be ready to bring some of the audience up on stage to sing with you. Give it a real party flavor."

The girls sat staring at Kyra.

"What? You don't think this is doable?" Kyra asked.

"No, it's totally doable," Tig said. "I think we're just really impressed by how good you are at all this."

"All what?" said Kyra.

"All the thinking through the details," said Tig.

"Oh," said Kyra. "I think it's fun. Besides, it gives me something to think about besides my parents. And hey, just because I can't play an instrument worth a flip doesn't mean I don't know what would make a good show. Ooh! You know what else I was thinking?

Y'all need a website or a social media page. Maybe both. Something the students and parents can go look at when someone brings up your name. Maybe a home page with a lot of red for the border? And maybe . . ." Kyra continued churning out ideas for marketing the band as the girls listened.

Robbie, Tig, Olivia, and Claire looked at one another while Kyra talked. They all seemed to be thinking the same thing: Who knew Kyra had such a head for this side of the music industry?

"I could set all that up for you," Kyra said. "If you want."

"We couldn't ask you to do that," Robbie said. Tig wondered if Robbie just wanted to make sure Kyra wouldn't do anything else to earn that percentage.

"I wouldn't mind at all," Kyra said. "I think it'd be fun."

By the end of the week, Pandora's Box had a social media page with more than three hundred followers.

"How'd you do that?" Tig asked Kyra one night on the phone.

"It wasn't hard," Kyra said. She explained how she'd targeted people who seemed likely to support the band, and then courted their interest. "What you do is, you find the people who have the most influence, and you go after them. Then other people just naturally follow whatever those people buy into, and before you know it, you have an audience."

"Thanks, Kyra," Tig said. She was so appreciative, she decided she felt generous enough to bring up Kyra's favorite subject and listen to her drone on, no matter how long it took. "What does Milo think of all this?"

"Oh, I don't know," Kyra said. "I haven't talked to him in a few days."

"You haven't?"

"No, we broke up."

"You broke up? When?"

"I can't remember, exactly. A couple of weekends ago?"

CHAPTER FORTY-EIGHT

"And you didn't tell me?" Tig asked.

"Nothing much to tell," Kyra said. "We're still friends and all. But as a boyfriend, he was kind of . . . well . . . exhausting. He expected us to talk every day. He thought I should come to all his extracurriculars. I swear, he was a bottomless pit. It got old kinda fast."

"Wow," said Tig.

"Wow what?"

"You surprise me sometimes, Kyra. I thought all you wanted in the world was a boyfriend."

"I used to. But all this with my folks . . . You know how Robbie's always going on about 'boyfriend girls'? She's got a point. You can put everything into another person and then wake up one day to find that they don't care about you anymore. I've watched it happen from a front-row seat. I guess it's just . . . I don't want my entire life to be about some guy. I want to find my own thing."

"Well, I think you've found it," Tig said.

After they hung up, Tig thought about how brave Kyra was being. If Kyra could be brave about something as big as her parents' divorce, maybe Tig could be brave about things in her life too.

She mustered the courage to send the text she'd been delaying all week.

You heard about Olivia and Will? she texted Paris.

Yep.

I had nothing to do with it. Promise.

I believe you.

Tig didn't know what else to say. A few minutes went by, and Paris texted again:

I'm not going to tell anyone. You can trust me.

Thanks, Tig replied.

Paris had been cool about everything else so far. Maybe she'd be cool about this, too.

Chapter Forty-Nine

"I liked your band's page," Regan said in algebra. "You're up to five hundred and something followers now. Your design is great! Did you pay somebody to do that?"

"Actually, Kyra did it," Tig said.

"Really?" said Regan. "I'm impressed. Hey, a little birdie told me that y'all are auditioning for West Al Academy's prom."

"Let me guess," said Tig. "A little birdie named Kyra?"

"No," Regan said. "A friend of mine at West Al.

Kyra hasn't really tried to talk to me in a while. I think she's over it."

Tig was both taken aback and proud. Maybe Kyra really had gotten the self-confidence she needed. Could it be that she'd actually given up chasing after the Bots? "She's been pretty busy with promoting the band," Tig said. "I think we're going to make her manager. Don't tell anyone, though. We want it to be a surprise when we ask her."

"Consider it in the vault," Regan said. "And speaking of items in the vault, how are things since the big breakup?"

"I'm not sure," Tig said. "Olivia is still pretty down about it, but I think she's getting a little better every day. We've been focusing pretty hard on the audition, so I think that's helped to take her mind off things."

"I meant with you and Will," said Regan. "He's free now; you're free. . . ."

"Oh, I couldn't," Tig said. "It's too soon to even think about anything like that. I wouldn't do that to Olivia, and neither would Will. In fact, I haven't even talked to him since they broke up, except just saying hello in the halls and in this class."

"I wouldn't leave him hanging for too long," Regan said. "That boy is getting cuter all the time. Somebody might swoop in, you know?"

Tig laughed. "I'm too busy with the band to worry about swooping."

Will came in and sat down. "Regan," he said. "Tig."

"Good day to you, sir," Regan replied.

Will smiled and shook his head.

"Guess who's auditioning for West Al Academy's prom," Regan said.

"Really?" Will asked. "That's cool."

"Cool is exactly what it is," Regan said. "This one right here? Cool, man. Cooooool."

Tig scrunched up her face and held up her palms. "What are you even doing, Regan?"

"Just trying to start some trouble, I guess." Regan smiled. Then she whispered to Tig, "Somebody has to get you two talking again. You're both afraid to breathe around each other!"

"What songs are you going to play at the audition?" Will asked.

"We've narrowed it down to a few we're trying to choose between," she said.

"If you need an outside opinion, you know, on the song choices," Will said, "I'd be glad to help. Maybe we could talk about them later or something."

"Maybe," said Tig.

That afternoon Tig thought about calling Will. She knew his remark in algebra about talking later had nothing to do with the song selections and everything to do with Olivia . . . or more specifically, what would happen now between the two of them.

But Tig wouldn't make the call. She felt disloyal to Olivia for even considering it.

It was almost four p.m. when her phone rang. The screen verified her gut feeling that it was Will.

"What's up?" he asked.

"Nothing," Tig said.

"Got a lot of homework tonight?"

"A little."

"Oh." Long pause. "Well, I'm glad we had this talk."

Tig laughed gently. "Yeah, me too."

"Olivia doesn't seem to be taking it too well," Will said. "The breakup, I mean. She won't even talk to me anymore."

"Give her time," Tig said. "It's a fresh wound."

"You're not mad at me, are you?"

"No," Tig said.

"At least there's that. I think the rest of Olivia's friends think I'm the devil."

"They don't," Tig said. "They're just trying to support Liv, which is good. Especially since I'm probably not doing the best job of it. I feel so guilty, I can hardly say anything to her."

"You don't have any reason to feel guilty," Will said. "Like I already told you: it's not your fault. You can't help it that you enticed me with your feminine wiles."

"My *what?*" Tig said.

Will started laughing. "What? Didn't you know

you had feminine wiles?"

"I'm not even sure what feminine wiles are, so no, I didn't know I had any."

"Well, you do," Will said. "Trust me on that."

"Listen, Will," Tig said. "No offense, but I don't think we should be talking right now. It's too soon. If I were to let it slip, something like, 'Will said on the phone that . . . ,' or whatever, it would be bad. Do you understand?"

"I understand," Will said. "I don't like it, but I understand. I want to be able to talk to you, but I can wait a little longer. I've waited this long, right?"

Tig was glad Will couldn't see her blush. "I've got to get to my drum lesson. Catch you later," she said, and hung up.

Traffic was terrible as usual on the way to the music store, so Tig was her typical five minutes late. But Lee was so excited to hear about the West Alabama Academy audition, he didn't even scold her.

"I can't believe you got an audition slot!" he said.

"I think we're getting attention based on the fact

that we're a bunch of little girls," Tig said. "It's not like we're as good as the other bands."

"Good enough and getting better," Lee said.

"We were thinking maybe 'Good Riddance' for a slow song and 'Blitzkrieg Bop' for a high-energy, jumping-around crowd-pleaser," Tig said.

"You know 'Good Riddance' doesn't have drums in the original version, I suppose?"

"I know," said Tig. "I worked out some fills and beats of my own for it. I want to keep it delicate, mostly some light cymbal work."

"Impressive," Lee said. "You'll be writing original material pretty soon. Let's hear what you've got."

Tig played her rendition for him. "Interesting," he said.

"Is it awful?"

"No, not at all," Lee replied. "It's just different to hear that song with drums. That's what makes art so stimulating, though; reimagining it in a variety of ways. I'm proud of you."

"Thanks," Tig said. "Can you walk me through

'Blitzkrieg Bop'?"

"Excellent choice," said Lee. "The big ol' guys who're embarrassed to dance will get out on the floor to jump around for that one."

"That's the plan," Tig said.

Tig loved the energy of that song, and it wasn't as hard as she thought it would be. Most of the work was on the bass and snare until the very end, when she played the low tom.

"Remember when you first started out and I forced you to use that metronome all the time?" Lee asked.

"Yes," Tig said.

"It paid off. Your rhythm is flawless."

Chapter Fifty

"I hope you ladies brought your A game, because Lee said my rhythm is flawless!" Tig announced at practice the next day.

"I thought your head seemed a little bigger than the last time I saw you," Paris joked.

The girls had decided to audition with "Blitzkrieg Bop" and "Good Riddance" to show their range, but the set list they'd present to the prom committee would include three Motown songs and some newer pop songs, plus all the previous songs they'd learned—even including the One Nothing piece Tig had sworn she'd never play again after the fiasco at Kyra's birthday party. If they wanted to fill three full hours, they couldn't be picky.

"I have an idea for a song," Olivia said. She began playing a slow, melancholy tune on the keyboard.

"I've heard that before," Robbie said. "But I can't put my finger on it. What is it?"

"Hey, I know," said Claire. "That's 'Now It's Dead,' isn't it?"

"Wait," Tig said. "That pop song?"

"Ewwww!" Robbie said. "Not just a pop song, but a poor-pitiful-me breakup song! Olivia, what are you thinking?"

"I think it's beautiful," Olivia replied.

"It's really not," Robbie said.

"Oh, Liv," Claire said. "It's because you're so hurt, isn't it?"

"This song says everything I feel right now," Olivia said, her eyes welling up. Claire hugged her.

"I'm sorry, Olivia," Tig said. "But come on, you know we can't play that song."

"Why not?" Olivia asked.

"Because it's just a really, really bad song," Robbie said. "I mean, seriously? The chorus compares their failed relationship to a dead armadillo on the side of the road."

"But that's what it feels like!" Olivia said. "You think you have this love that's so strong, you know? And nothing can penetrate it. And then, the next thing you know, smash! Your love is dead and it's just lying there, feet up, for everyone to look at as they drive past!"

Oh, brother! Tig thought.

Robbie couldn't persuade Olivia that the song was a stinker, so the girls had to take a vote on whether they'd try to add it to the set list. It was three to two, with Robbie, Tig, and Paris voting against and Olivia and Claire voting for. Claire had to admit, though, that even she didn't like the song; she was just trying to be supportive. For poor Olivia. Poor, sweet Olivia, who had been all but destroyed by the evil Will. Tig wasn't sure how much more of this she could take.

Luckily, Kyra came by after the song vote had been

taken. Since she generally liked terrible pop songs, and since her own parents' love had so recently become a dead armadillo, she might have thrown her support behind Olivia too. But the vote was over when she arrived, so Kyra instead offered advice on how the girls could move during the songs to make the show more appealing.

After two straight hours of practice, the girls called it a day. Homework and tests didn't stop just because they had a big audition. They'd practiced two hours a day every day that week in spite of their school commitments.

"I'm proud of us," Tig said. "We've worked hard, and we're going to have to work even harder if we actually get the gig, but I think we're ready for the audition tomorrow." Tig's phone rang. She looked at the screen. It was her uncle Paul. "Give me a second, y'all," she said.

"Hey, Uncle Paul," Tig said. "What's up?"

"Are you at band practice right now?" he asked.

"Yes, as a matter of fact," said Tig.

"Great," he replied. "Put me on speaker. I want all the girls to hear this."

"Listen up, everybody," Tig said, turning her phone on speaker. "We're all listening, Uncle Paul."

"I've got big news," he said. "Incredible, really. Unprecedented, in fact."

"What is it?" Tig asked.

"The commercial? The fake one? Well, when it went to nationals, the client had the deciding vote. The pants the commercial advertises are fake, of course, but the client is real."

"We know," Tig said. "Everybody shops there. But what's the big news?"

"The news is that the client absolutely loved the fake commercial. So much so that they want to feature you girls in a real one."

The girls looked at one another, gasped, and then began squealing and jumping up and down.

"Are you for real?" Tig asked.

"Very for real," Uncle Paul said.

"Are they going to fly us to New York to make a

commercial?" Robbie said.

"They'll probably film it here in town to keep costs down," Tig's uncle said. "But they plan to release the commercial nationally."

"That's amazing!" said Claire.

"I can't believe this!" said Olivia. "We're going to be on national TV!"

"We?" asked Paris. "Or y'all?"

Everyone stopped for a moment to ponder Paris's question. Then they looked at Kyra. "I'm not in the band anymore," said Kyra.

"Uncle Paul," said Tig, "Paris is our new bass player. What does that mean for the commercial?"

"Hmmm," said her uncle. "I'm not really sure. It would be up to the client." He promised to talk to his contact as soon as possible and let them know. "Go ahead and send me a photo and a short video of the new lineup. They'll want to see if they like Paris's look. I know that sounds shallow, but it is a visual medium. It matters."

"How could anyone not like her looks?" Tig said.

"I'll send you a pic. She's gorgeous." Paris blushed.

"Just got the picture. Looking at it right now. She's a pretty girl, yes," Uncle Paul said. "But she looks older than the rest of you. The client may think she looks too mature. You never know. Just send the video, okay?"

The girls agreed and then hung up. "Kyra," Tig said, "I don't know what to say. I know you were in the original commercial, but I don't want to be unfair to Paris."

"It's all right," said Kyra. "I mean, would I love to be on TV? Yeah. I'd be lying if I said no. But you have to think long-term. This will be nationwide exposure for Pandora's Box. If it takes off, you'll get offers for appearances, and who knows? Maybe even a record deal. As much as I'd like to be, I'm just not enough of a musician to keep up with all that. I'd only drag the band down. You know that and I know it."

Tig was stunned at how mature Kyra was being about all this. She wasn't sure she could've done the same in her place.

"Besides," Kyra said, "I'm sure the client will approve of Paris. They're after the all-girl band novelty. Replacing one girl bass player with another isn't that big of a deal."

"It's a big deal for you, though," said Robbie. "You sure you're okay with this?"

"Hey, I'm not saying I'm thrilled about it," Kyra replied. "But like I've told Tig, I've made peace with the fact that I'm not a musician. You five are. So just do your thing and let me ride your coattails, all right?" She smiled.

"We've got to make a video for the client," Paris said.

"I can get one tomorrow of y'all at the West Al audition," Kyra said. "No problem."

"The audition," Tig said. "As much as I'd like to wrap my head around all this with the commercial, we'd better keep our minds on that audition. I don't want to blow it."

The girls agreed: audition first, commercial next.

Chapter Fifty-One

Stage outfits were a big deal twice over this time. The girls wanted to impress the West Al people, but they also needed to look cool in the video Kyra would be shooting. Since they didn't know what sort of clothes the commercial might be selling, Kyra had suggested they all go in different fashion directions. That way, the client could envision multiple options and decide on the vibe they wanted once the time came to shoot the commercial.

Olivia wore a pink linen dress, which wouldn't have looked at all right for the occasion except for the fact that Olivia was so willowy that the spaghetti straps and the giant silver earrings framed her beautiful collarbone. Tig couldn't exactly do a dress or skirt while playing drums, so she opted for floral shorts and a loosely crocheted sweater and tank. Paris mixed a striped, short-sleeved sweater with a leopard print skirt. Robbie opted for an uncharacteristically romantic hippie look, with a flowy top and long, untied scarf with shorts, knee socks, and booties, but she gave it an edge with a big metal bracelet. Claire kept it simple with cuffed boyfriend jeans and a bulky black sweater, her hair decidedly undone and wispy to capture the laid-back feel of her ensemble.

They arrived at the West Al Academy auditorium the next afternoon just in time to see the end of another band's audition.

"That's New Haircut. I've heard of them," Robbie said. "They're awesome."

New Haircut—all college students—had six musicians and two female backup singers in addition to the lead. The backup singers also did choreography.

And quite well. They were just finishing up the Ike and Tina Turner version of "Proud Mary" when the girls arrived.

"I'm nauseated at how good that was," Olivia said to Tig. "We are so out of our league."

Tig couldn't form the words to reply. Olivia was exactly right.

"Look at this," Claire said. She picked up a piece of paper that had been left in a stack on one of the back chairs. It was the other band's set list . . . except that it really wasn't a set list, per se. Instead the top of the page said, *New Haircut: Samplings*. There were about fifty songs.

"They know so many songs, this is just a sampling!" Claire said. "We are so doomed."

"We're never going to get this gig," Paris said. "And I can live with that. But what do you say we just sneak out quietly right now so we don't humiliate ourselves?"

"Positive thinking!" Kyra said. "Besides, I've got to get a video for the commercial people, and where else are we going to get stage lighting and such a good setup? Just do your best."

The prom committee members stood up and cheered when the other band finished their song. "That was awesome," said a high-school boy who seemed to be in charge.

"Thank you," said a girl. "Your demo tape was excellent, but it does help us a lot to see how you come across live."

As New Haircut packed up their instruments and left the stage, the boy called, "Pandora's Box?"

Tig was sure she'd throw up, but she managed to say, "We're here."

"Great," said the boy. "We'll give you a couple of minutes to set up."

The girls opened with "Blitzkrieg Bop," which went off without a hitch. Then, without a pause, they moved into "Good Riddance." Tig thought both songs went well. At least the video for the commercial client would be good, even though they'd never get the prom gig.

"Your set list," the boy said. "Is this a sampling or

a complete, exhaustive list?"

Tig wanted to bluff, but she knew bluffing was the same as lying. And hadn't she done plenty of lying in the last few months? She thought of how lies had a habit of coming back to bite her. "We're a new band, obviously," Tig said. "So those are all the songs we know."

The boy nodded. Then the girl asked, "So, if someone wanted to make a request, what would you do?"

"I guess we'd have to be honest and tell them we couldn't do it," Tig said. If honesty was supposed to be the best policy, why did it feel so humiliating?

"Thank you for your time," the boy said. "We'll be in touch."

As the girls packed up their equipment, they noticed Kyra going over to the committee's table and whispering something to the group.

"What's she doing?" Robbie asked Tig.

"Probably apologizing," Tig replied. "What were we thinking? We're so not ready for the West Al prom!"

"Aren't you glad we didn't ask Kyra to be our manager?" Robbie said. "This was her big idea, after all. She's overly confident."

"I suppose so," Tig said. "Man, I would've loved to have gotten this prom!"

"Maybe one day," Robbie said.

Tig's mom took the girls out for pizza after the audition. They commiserated about how embarrassing it was to have to go on after New Haircut.

"If we are this pizza," Robbie said, "New Haircut is filet mignon."

"If New Haircut is a Porsche," said Olivia, "we're my dad's old, dinged-up pickup truck."

"They're Godiva chocolate," said Claire, "and we're those rubbery, pale orange peanut things no one eats."

"Circus peanuts," said Tig.

"Right!" said Claire. "We're circus peanuts."

"I like circus peanuts," said Paris.

"I suppose they serve their purpose," said Tig. "They're a novelty. But there's not much to them. It's a good comparison."

"Stop whining," Kyra said. "Y'all had a great audition! You didn't miss a note!"

"Oh, but when the committee chairman asked about requests!" said Robbie. "Didn't you just want to climb under a rock?" They all agreed.

"Well, if I could play as well as y'all do," Kyra said, "I wouldn't hide anywhere. I'd be proud. And you all should be too." Kyra's phone rang. "I have to take this."

"Probably Milo," said Robbie.

"They broke up. Didn't I tell you?" asked Tig.

"No," said Robbie. "Milo dumped her?"

"I think she dumped him," said Tig.

"She did," Paris said. "Milo told me about it at school. They're still friends, though."

"No one tells me anything," said Robbie.

"I guess we've been too concerned with the audition to think about Kyra's love life," said Olivia. "And mine."

"Olivia, we're so sorry!" said Claire. "We've been

insensitive, haven't we? It's been a few days since I've asked how you were doing."

"I'm glad no one's asked," said Olivia. "It's helped. I think I'm getting over it. Like Tig said, all this practice for the audition hasn't left room for thinking about much else. And that's been a good thing."

Kyra came back to the table. "What'd I miss?" she asked.

"Nothing much," said Tig. "Who was that?"

"Just the West Al Academy prom committee chairman," said Kyra.

The girls groaned.

"The big 'thanks but no thanks'?" Tig asked.

"Not exactly," said Kyra. "You kinda got the job."

"Right," Robbie said. "And also, we just won the lottery."

"I'm serious," said Kyra. "You kinda got the job."

The girls all began talking at once, asking questions about how, why, and what about New Haircut?

"Hold up," Tig said. "What do you mean we *kinda* got the job?"

"I mean, it wasn't exactly what you had in mind," Kyra said. "And the pay isn't going to be three thousand dollars."

"Kyra!" Tig said. "Spit it out! What's going on?"

"Pandora's Box is going to be the warm-up act," Kyra explained. "You'll play your set list before New Haircut performs for the rest of the evening. Your pay is going to be three hundred and fifty dollars, total. Not per person. But I did get them to agree to having your favorite snacks in the dressing room: peanut-butter-filled pretzels for Robbie, ginger ale for Claire, and barbeque chips for Tig and Paris. I didn't specify for Olivia because, come on, what *doesn't* she eat?"

No one said anything.

"You're upset?" Kyra asked. "Look, I can ask for those ice pops she likes if they have a freezer close by. . . ."

"No," Tig said.

Before Tig could finish her thought, Kyra added, "Well, if it's the money you're upset about, just remember that the exposure and the prestige of West

Alabama Academy's prom is worth something too, and—"

"Nobody's upset!" Tig said. "We're just kind of shocked. How did you do it?"

"After the audition, I told them about how you'd done opening-act gigs before. Then I told them about the commercial," Kyra said. "They'd already seen your social media page and how it's blowing up with fans. The commercial cinched it. How could they pass up being the first prom to showcase a rising national talent? And maybe the last. I told them that after the commercial airs, you guys might not be playing proms anymore. This was probably their only chance to ever book you."

"You're unbelievable," said Tig. "How did you know how to do all this?"

"I don't know," Kyra said. "It comes kind of naturally. Sort of like the way drums are for you. It's fun! Making deals is a rush!"

"Would you excuse us one moment?" Tig asked. She and the other girls walked away from the table to confer. They were unanimous. When they came back to the table, Tig said, "Kyra, we'd like to officially ask you to be the manager for Pandora's Box."

"Really?" said Kyra. "Thanks. But what exactly does a manager do?"

"You manage us," Robbie said. "Just like you've already been doing."

"And you make fifteen percent of whatever we make," said Tig.

"You're serious?" Kyra said.

"Dead serious," said Tig.

"Yes!" said Kyra. "A thousand times yes!"

There were hugs and squeals, and then Kyra pulled out her phone again. She typed in something and exclaimed, "You do realize this would cut each of your pay to just under sixty dollars instead of seventy."

"Totally worth it," Claire said. "If it weren't for you, we wouldn't have any money at all."

"Or the West Al prom!" Olivia said.

Robbie looked at Tig and grimaced a bit. Then she smiled and said, "Claire's right. Totally worth it."

Three days later, after receiving the video Kyra made, Uncle Paul got word from the client.

Paris would be just fine. . . .

The commercial was a go!

Everything in Tig's life seemed to be falling into place.

Chapter Fifty-Two

The following Monday at school, it seemed that word had gotten out about Pandora's Box getting the prom gig. In the gym before the first bell, the girls got several congratulations from different classmates. When the bell rang and they all began to file out of the gym, Tig realized she'd left her lunch bag on the bleachers. "Shoot," she said to her group. "Be right back."

Trying to get back into the gym while everyone else was leaving was like swimming upstream, of course. Just as she'd finally gotten past the doors, someone pulled her arm and tugged her toward the wall. Instinctively, Tig pulled back, until she looked up and saw that it was Will.

"Oh, hey," she said.

"I just wanted to get you alone for a second," Will said.

Tig looked around at all the other students exiting the gym. "This is alone?"

Will smiled. "It will be in about a minute. Listen, I just heard about the prom gig. That's really great. I'm proud of you."

Tig blushed. "Thanks."

"You're pretty amazing. You know that?"

"Will . . . ," Tig began. She looked down. Will's hand found her chin and gently pulled it up. Their eyes met. Then he brushed her bangs out of her eyes.

"We can't do this right now," Tig said.

"You're right. We don't want to be late for class."

"No, I don't mean 'this' as in the two of us talking, right here, right now. I mean 'this' as in us . . . you and me . . . together. The timing's not right."

Will sighed. "When will the timing be right?"

"I think we need to at least finish out the school year, don't you? Give Olivia some time to get over you?"

"So the day after school gets out?" He smiled. "Not that I'm overly eager or anything."

"Let's play it by ear," Tig said. "This summer will give everybody some space . . . and some time to figure things out."

"You're right," Will said. "In the meantime, you kill it at that prom. I'm rooting for you."

Tig smiled. "Killing it is exactly what we plan to do."

Chapter Fifty-Three

At one of the last few rehearsals before the prom, after they'd run through the full set list and were about to call it a day, Paris said, "I know we've learned a lot of new songs lately, and I may be way off base even suggesting this, but I've got an idea."

Everyone stopped packing up and gave Paris their attention. "Robbie, you got something to go with this?" Paris started playing a bass line, a wicked grin spreading across her face.

"Ahhh!" Robbie exclaimed. "You know I do!" Robbie started playing along on the guitar.

"*Yes!*" said Tig. She began pounding out an appropriate drumbeat.

"I can deal with this," said Olivia. "I love this song!" She fell in on keyboards.

After they'd grooved a few bars, Claire jumped in with the lyrics.

When it was over, the girls all yelled and high-fived.

"Why didn't we think of this a long time ago?" Robbie said.

"I know!" said Tig. "This is the perfect song for us! Good call, P!"

"You know what we should do?" Claire said. "Do it for our encore at prom."

"It'll bring down the house!" said Olivia. "This song is our secret weapon!"

"I'll get dozens of balloons to come down from the ceiling when the song begins!" Kyra said. "I'll pass out cans of that spray string! Oh, the crowd will go absolutely wild! How totally fun!"

Tig smiled, thinking of how the West Al Academy prom would be a night no one would soon forget.

Chapter Fifty-Four

One thing about West Alabama Academy: they knew how to do prom right.

"The yacht club," Paris said. "Fancy folks. I never thought I'd be playing music here."

"This is nothing," Robbie said. "Next month you'll be shooting a national commercial. Bet you didn't see that coming either."

"Can't say I did," Paris replied.

"Stick with me, kid," Robbie said. "I can take you places."

In the dressing room, the girls found the peanut-butter pretzels, ginger ale, and barbeque chips, just as Kyra had promised. The girl from the prom committee stopped by to see if the girls needed anything else before they went on. "No, thanks," Tig said. "We're great. I mean, not like, 'We're great' like we think we're great or something—"

"We have everything we need," Robbie said, shaking her head at Tig.

The girls put the finishing touches on their stage looks. Robbie wore spandex pants and a patterned top; Olivia, a graphic tee, jean shorts over purple leggings with combat boots, and a knit beanie; Tig, a plaid peplum top and jeans; Paris, a black leather skirt and black top with a big necklace; and Claire, neon glow-in-the-dark bracelets and black leather pants with a white T-shirt with black stars.

When they were situated on the stage and the lights were still down, Tig could hear the murmur and shuffling of the crowd. It made her nervous, but also excited. When the prom committee chairman said, "Ladies and gentlemen, Pandora's Box!" Robbie gave a quick nod to Tig before they launched into "Blitz-krieg Bop." That upbeat tune went over big with the already enthusiastic crowd. Parents, teachers, and all the students were on the floor jumping all over the place. No one was hanging back. The crowd cheered the end of that song as the girls seamlessly segued into "It's Only Rock 'n Roll."

Next they launched into "Signed, Sealed, Delivered," followed by the One Nothing song Tig had feared she would mess up. But surprisingly, it wasn't Tig who flubbed . . . it was Robbie. During the intro, Robbie missed a half step, which threw her off on the drop. She picked it back up in the chorus, though. She turned around and looked at Tig and stuck out her tongue and squeezed her eyes shut. Then they both smiled and nodded at each other. Tig was kind of relieved to see that even Robbie could have an off moment once in a while.

When Claire thanked the crowd and said good night, the girls listened as the audience clapped and requested more. They waited only a minute or two before the encore. There were cheers and whistles when they returned to the stage.

"I hope you all had fun tonight!" Claire said. The crowd whooped. "I know we had fun. And you know. . . ." Claire began slowly singing the title verse of the iconic chorus without musical accompaniment. Even though she sang it drawn out and dramatically, without its customary bounciness, the audience knew what was coming next and went absolutely berserk.

When the band struck up "Girls Just Want to Have Fun," the floor was packed with more dancers than before. As Kyra had promised, balloons came down from the ceiling, and the students, teachers, and parents all squealed as they danced around and sprayed one another using the cans of spray string.

As Pandora's Box packed up and New Haircut set up, the prom chairman piped music from his phone through the speakers to tide the crowd over. Mrs. Marquez handed Kyra a check. "You ladies did not disappoint," she said. "Thank you for an excellent opening act!"

"Our pleasure," Kyra said. "Thank *you*."

"Such big things ahead for you girls! National exposure! Who knows what might result? I'm really looking forward to your commercial!" Mrs. Marquez said.

The girls, tired but still racing with adrenaline from a great set, smiled.

"Thanks. So are we," Tig said. "So are we."

About the Author

Ginger Rue is the author of *Brand-New Emily* and *Jump*. She's a former advice columnist for a teen magazine, and her work has appeared in *Seventeen*, *Teen Vogue*, *Girls' Life*, *Family Circle*, and other publications. She is currently a contributing editor for *Guideposts*.

Ginger lives in Tuscaloosa, Alabama, with her husband, two daughters, and stepson. Before becoming a writer, Ginger toured extensively with Van Halen as their backup drummer. Okay, so she can't play drums at all and she totally made up the part about touring with Van Halen... but she's a fiction writer, so making stuff up is her job.